# Finding Franklin

## *Mystery of the Lost State Capitol*

## JOE TENNIS

The vintage postcard of Bristol Caverns appears courtesy of Shelby Edwards and Tim Buchanan. The photo-illustration of "The Miners of Silver Dollar City" appears courtesy of Dollywood. The image of the original Lost State of Franklin capitol appears courtesy of the Greeneville-Greene County Library. All other photo-illustrations are by the author.

This book is a work of fiction.
Names, places, characters, and incidents are products of the author's imagination or are used fictitiously.

ISBN 13: 978-1719534994
ISBN 10: 1719534993
Copyright © 2011, 2018 by Joe Tennis
All Rights Reserved
Printed in the United States of America

2 3 4 5 6 7 8 9 0

*For Thomas, Amber, and Ben*

# ACKNOWLEDGMENTS

Foremost thanks to my publishers, Daniel Lewis and Victoria Fletcher; my editor, Sherry Lewis; my wife, Mary; and most especially my daughter, Abigail, who consistently inspired me with ideas and endured road trips in search of "treasures" across North Carolina, Tennessee, and Virginia.

Several historians, colleagues, and friends also helped along the way, including Carol Jackson, V. N. "Bud" Phillips, Faith Stahl, Archer Blevins, Donna Fee, Billy Dixon, Beth Wright, Karin O'Brien, Shirley Adair, June Presley, Linda Hoagland, Daniel Rodgers, Mike West, Shelby Edwards, Tim Buchanan, George Stone, Jan Patrick, Rex and Lisa McCarty, Bonnie Roberts Erickson, Jo Hutton, Judith L. Hurwitz, Carol Borneman, Earl Fletcher, Cara Ellen Modisett, Donnamarie Emmert, Judy Roher, Josh Balthis, Brenda Sullins, Tim Cable, Gary and MaryGrace Walrath, Jess Bolling, Bill McKee, Ken Heath, Bob and Suzy Harrison, Christina Gordon, Jean Kilgore, Patsy Phillips, Sandra Fisher, Rick Wagner, David McGee, Trish McGee, Pete Owens, Ashley Adams, Betty Thomas, Kathryn Nichols, Andrea Cheak, Craig Distl, The Peanut Patch of Courtland, Virginia, and the staff of the Franklin Gem & Mineral Museum in Franklin, North Carolina.

I also want to thank family members for their support and encouragement: Maggie Caudill; Pat and Angie Wolfe; Sam Caudill; Melissa Caudill; Ralph Boswell; Jo Boswell; John Wolfe; Rob Tennis; my parents, Richard and Jeanette Tennis; and my son, John Patrick.

# CONTENTS

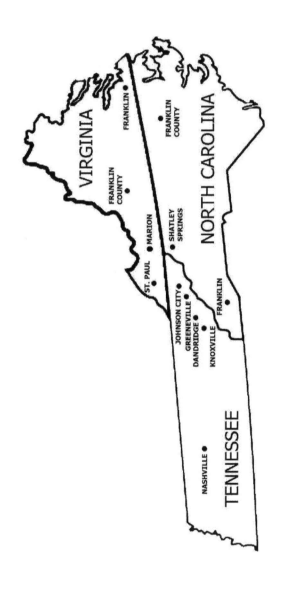

VIRGINIA

FRANKLIN

FRANKLIN
COUNTY

FRANKLIN
COUNTY

MARION

SHATLEY
SPRINGS

ST. PAUL

NORTH CAROLINA

JOHNSON CITY
GREENEVILLE
DANDRIDGE
KNOXVILLE

FRANKLIN

TENNESSEE

NASHVILLE

# NOLICHUCKY RIVER, TENNESSEE
## *Treasury*

It must have been the hottest day of summer as Thomas and Zakk stood on the banks of the Nolichucky River. The two young cousins had come to fish near Greeneville, Tennessee, with their uncle, Big Jon.

A big man, Big Jon drove a tiny blue pickup he called "The Little Ranger." He never drove fast. He always drove slow—so slow that he felt like he owned the road.

Armed with an arsenal of fishing rods, Big Jon arrived at his grandfather's favorite fishing hole on the Nolichucky, aiming to wage war on ass and bluegill. "You boys watch," Big Jon told his nephews, "and the master will show you."

At 35, Big Jon had a rounded look, much like a scruffy teddy bear, sporting a five o'clock shadow, a baseball cap, and a NASCAR t-shirt. His oldest nephew, Thomas, ten years old, had sandy hair and wore glasses. Nine-year-old Zakk--nicknamed "Zippy" because he moved fast—wore a crop of blond hair that Big Jon liked to call "a bowl cut."

This weekday afternoon marked the third of ten summer vacation days that the cousins planned to spend with Big Jon, their bachelor uncle, while Zakk's and Thomas's parents traveled across Colorado.

Zakk caught a tiny bluegill on his fishing rod. Next, Thomas pulled in a rock bass. And Big Jon? Well, he got his line snagged. Then his bobber flipped onto a rock.

Zakk said, "Sounds like you're playing Ping-Pong."

After that, Big Jon cut his line and spent the next half hour trying to get several knots out of his reel.

Then, all of a sudden, Zakk seemed to slip off the muddy riverbank.

"Hold on!" Big Jon hollered. "I'll get you!"

# SPLASH!

Big Jon flopped—clothes and all—into a shallow section of the river. He stood with water only up to his knees, yet he flailed his arms wildly, looking like a lost duck. Zakk laughed, and so did Thomas, as Big Jon just kept splashing. He had gotten his hair wet and all of his clothes. And he was embarrassed. His fishing pole had slipped out of his hand and drifted down the river.

"What happened?" Zakk asked. "I was reaching to swat a mosquito."

"Err," Big Jon growled then spat a stream of water out of his mouth and onto Zakk.

Climbing back toward the bank, Big Jon pushed his right hand into the squishy mud, and it sank. The mud climbed almost to his elbow.

"Ow!" Big Jon hollered. "What the—"

"Huh?" Thomas said.

"I touched something," Big Jon said. "Down in the mud."

"Where, sir?" Thomas asked.

"Right there. Dig for it," Big Jon ordered, stepping back on land. "It's some kind of something."

Thomas carefully placed his fishing pole in the grass. Then he picked up a rock and used it like a shovel to dig in the mud. Zakk soon joined in, scooping out more mud with a squashed soda can. Within a few minutes, the boys unearthed a square board about a foot long and a foot wide.

By this time, Big Jon had wandered several yards from the river, all the time holding his right thumb and complaining about that hidden "something."

"What do you think this is?" Zakk asked.

"It says something," Thomas said, clearing mud from the board.

Within minutes, the boys had found their answer. Engraved on the waterlogged wood were black letters, considerably faded, but clearly spelling: "FRANKLIN TREASURY."

"Treasury?" Zakk asked. "What's a treasury?"

It might be a treasure," Thomas said. "What do you think, Big Jon?"

"Err," Big Jon growled. "I think that dumb board gave me a splinter."

"Well, it might mean something," Thomas said. "It's like a mystery. It's old looking, sir. Very old."

"Well, throw it in the back of the Little Ranger and take it home," Big Jon commanded. "It's almost time for supper."

"Now, sir?" Thomas asked.

"But what about the fish?" Zakk said. "Aren't we gonna keep fishing?"

"Heh-heh," Big Jon said. "I, uh, I think, I, uh… I think I've caught my limit."

# GREENEVILLE, TENNESSEE
## *Lost Capitol*

Just as soon as Big Jon made it back home a few miles, Thomas grabbed the "FRANKLIN TREASURY" sign and headed into the two-story farmhouse.

Big Jon had inherited the farmhouse from his grandfather, a country doctor the whole family had called "Papaw." It sat on a hill near Mount Hebron, not far from downtown Greeneville, Tennessee.

About an hour after the fishing trip, Big Jon fixed hot dogs and asked his neighbor Old Man Dan to come over for supper.

"I knew your great-grandfather," Old Man Dan told Thomas and Zakk. "Your papaw and I even shared a few secrets."

"Really?" Thomas said.

"Sure," Old Man Dan said. "People tell secrets to their doctors all the time."

"What kind of secrets?" Zakk asked.

"Oh, maybe what hurts their leg, what made 'em sick," Old Man Dan said, smiling.

Zakk signed and said, "Those secrets are boring."

"Boring?" Old Man Dan grinned. "Oh, but people would also tell of treasures, scattered among the stones and bluffs of the valley."

"Treasures?" Thomas asked.

"Wait a minute," Zakk interjected, speaking with half a hot dog in his mouth. "How old are you, Mr. Dan?"

"Why, old!" Old Man Dan said, leaning into Zakk's nine-year-old face. "Last recall, I was nearing 102 years old. Why, that's almost a century beyond you boys."

"A century?" Zakk asked.

"Treasures?" Thomas asked again.

Old Man Dan laughed and said, "Boys, lost fortunes are everywhere—silver mines, pots of gold. Some people buried all they had to keep it safe during the Depression. And some people had their fortunes stolen and thrown into the caves."

"Caves?" Zakk said.

Immediately, Thomas ran to retrieve the FRANKLIN TREASURY board from another room. He ran back and handed it to Old Man Dan. Panting, Thomas asked, "What's this, sir? What do you think this is?"

Rubbing his worn and wrinkled fingers across the letters, Old Man Dan studied the board carefully.

"Don't touch it too hard," Big Jon said. "That dumb thing gave me a splinter."

Old Man Dan began to smile. "Where did you get this?" he said, looking at Thomas.

"In the mud," Big Jon said.

"We went fishing on the Nolichucky River," Zakk added. "And it was the only thing that Big Jon caught."

Old Man Dan laughed and said, "This is from Franklin. Has to be."

"Franklin?" Thomas asked.

"Ben Franklin?" Big Jon said. "What? That old coot with the kite and the key?"

"He was an inventor," Thomas said, still panting.

Zakk smiled and said, "Isn't Ben Franklin the man on the $100 bill?"

"Yes, young man, that's Benjamin Franklin. And this might be from Franklin." Old Man Dan nodded his bald head. "I'll bet this is part of ol' Ben Franklin's lost state."

"Lost state?" Thomas wondered.

Old Man Dan grinned. "From the looks of this board, I think you must have found a piece of the old capitol building— the one that's been missing all these years, ever since even before I was born."

"Before you were born?" Zakk said. "Man, you so old.... What, like when the dinosaurs was around?"

"No," Old Man Dan said, almost agitated. "I'm talking about 1896 and 1897. Tennessee turned 100 years old, and they took this old cabin from down here in Greeneville, and they sent it to Nashville."

"Nashville?" Zakk said. "That's where Hannah Montana is from."

Thomas, ignoring Zakk, looked at Old Man Dan and asked, "What was in the cabin?"

"Well, it was the capitol building for the Lost State of Franklin," Old Man Dan said. "At least, we always believed that it was. And Greeneville was the capital of it all."

Thomas stood, confused, not saying a word.

"Look," Old Man Dan said. "Before there was a Tennessee, when the United States was just a-forming, there was this state, and they called it Franklin—back in the 1780s. People were living here, all in these valleys, and here in Greeneville, and they were part of North Carolina. But, then, North Carolina didn't want them anymore. So they formed their own state."

"And they named it for Benjamin Franklin? Thomas asked.

"That's right," Old Man Dan said. "Only it never got to actually being a real state. Not really. Franklin was around for a few years, but then it got lost. And then so did the capitol building."

"It got lost?" Zakk said.

"They had the old cabin torn down here and shipped off to Nashville," Old Man Dan said. "They had celebrated Tennessee being 100 years old, and they wanted Franklin to be part of the celebration. And then? Well, somebody lost the building. Or somebody stole the building. Or something happened. That old building just never came back home here to Greeneville."

"So the Lost State of Franklin lost its capitol building?" Thomas said.

Old Man Dan nodded. "All us old-timers used to talk about where it went off to—and was there anything inside?"

"Like a treasure? Or a fortune?" Thomas asked

"Or maybe just this treasury," Old Man Dan said, tapping his right index finger on the FRANKLIN TREASURY sign.

Big Jon got in Old Man Dan's face and said, "What's this thing downtown?"

"What?"

"Down there by the spring with all the crawfish," Big Jon said. "In Greeneville, there's some old cabin that says 'Franklin' on it."

"Oh, that's the replica of the lost capitol building," Old Man Dan said, nodding. "That's just make-believe. People around Greeneville, they wanted something. So they built that to remind everybody that this place used to be part of Franklin."

"And the treasure?" Thomas said, his eyes bugging out.

Old Man Dan laughed and stood up. He handed the FRANKLIN TREASURY sign back to Thomas and then propped himself on his cane. "I don't know about a treasure, but wait a minute." Old Man Dan reached into his pocket and fiddled with his keys. He pulled one off his key chain and handed it to Thomas, saying, "Take this."

"This?" Thomas asked.

"It's something y'all's papaw gave me, long time ago," Old Man Dan said. "I was in his doctor's office, and he passed this on to me. He never did say what it was for. But now's as good a time as any to give it to one of you."

"Thank you, sir," Thomas said.

"Well, who knows?" Old Man Dan said, just before he walked away and went home. "Maybe you can take this key or that sign and find a Franklin fortune."

# JOHNSON CITY, TENNESSEE
## *Dark and Bloody Ground*

Thomas hardly slept that night. Constantly muttering the words *Franklin fortune*, he stayed awake until the wee hours of the morning, going through every old Tennessee history book in the farmhouse, looking for clues to what he thought was a mystery.

He skimmed Papaw's history books and jotted down notes about Franklin. He also surfed the Internet and printed off so many articles about the State of Franklin that he ran out of paper and broke Big Jon's printer.

As Thomas discovered, Old Man Dan was right. A state called "Franklin" had existed from 1784 to 1788 in present-day Northeast Tennessee. Greeneville served as Franklin's capital for three years. But what happened to the original capitol building?

Well, what everyone had assumed was the actual capitol disappeared, just like Old Man Dan had said. The cabin was moved by barge to Nashville, and it never came back.

So was there a fortune left behind? Oh, Thomas could only wonder.

The next morning, Thomas yawned. He was tired. Still, he was anxious as he joined the breakfast table; Big Jon had fixed bacon and eggs.

"Big day," Big Jon said. "Going to Johnson City to my favorite restaurant. Gonna get me some chicken."

"Johnson City?" Thomas said. "Here? In Tennessee? Johnson City? We have to go there, sir. And some other places. That's one of Franklin's hot spots. We can find the Franklin fortune."

"Franklin?" Big Jon said, scrunching up his face. "What do you mean, Franklin? What is that? All that stuff that Old Man Dan said?"

"He's right," Thomas said, speaking fast. "He's doubly

right. I did all the research. There was a Franklin, sir. And that board we found must be a clue."

"Err," Big Jon growled. "All that board did for me is give me a sore thumb."

"You still have a splinter?" Zakk asked as he slurped some milk.

Big Jon held up this thumb dramatically, and Zakk laughed.

An hour later, the trio drove into Greeneville and discovered the replica of the Lost State of Franklin capitol building, constructed in 1966, just about a block off Main Street. The cabin was unlocked, and Zakk led the charge to go upstairs. "It's spooky," he said.

*Replica of the Lost State of Franklin's capitol building.*

Thomas, meanwhile, studied every part of the two-story structure, taking measurements with a ruler and snapping pictures with a camera. He paced the stone steps outside the cabin, too, and he imagined what it was like for Franklin's leaders to challenge authority and form their own state—here, in what had been North Carolina in the 1780s.

Later, holding on to his tattered pile of notes, Thomas asked Big Jon to stop at a state park in Limestone, Tennessee, so they could study another log cabin: It was a replica of the birthplace of Davy Crockett, a famed frontiersman who was born when Limestone was part of the State of Franklin.

A half-hour later, Big Jon slowly cruised into Jonesborough, Tennessee. And here, in a downtown corridor of well-preserved, antique buildings, Thomas took a picture of a monument outside the Washington County Courthouse. An inscription noted Jonesborough had served as the capital of the State of Franklin—before Greeneville.

Still, while standing on a sidewalk, Zakk acted scared and said, "I think we oughta leave."

"Why?" Thomas asked.

"Because there's a ghost here," Zakk said. "I read in a book that there was a ghost of Andrew Jackson here. The president, Andrew Jackson. He walks up and down Main Street. He's a ghost, and he's a—"

"Boo!" Big Jon suddenly said, appearing at Zakk's back and causing Zakk to scream and Thomas's glasses to fall off his face.

"Zippy Zakk got zapped!" Big Jon laughed heartily. "Are you boys hungry?" he asked.

"I'm starving, sir," Thomas said.

"Me too," Zakk added.

In another 30 minutes, Big Jon pulled into the parking lot of an orange-and-white restaurant in Johnson City, a sprawling city with several stores and restaurants.

After giving the waitress an order for a big plate of chicken wings, Big Jon looked at the door and saw his younger brother, Bob, a 31-year-old man with fuzzy hair. Thomas and Zakk knew him best as "Uncle Pickle," a nickname he got because he always wore green. Also coming through the door was Uncle Pickle's five-year-old daughter—Thomas and Zakk's cousin—a blonde-haired girl named AnnaBelle. She wore a polka-dot dress and carried a doll she called "Miss Brenda."

Uncle Pickle and AnnaBelle sat down at the table with Big

Jon, Thomas, and Zakk. Before long, the waitress brought their food, and they dug in.

"We're on a mission," Big Jon announced sarcastically between bites. "Thomas thinks we're going to find some lost fortune."

Uncle Pickle, dressed in a green shirt, of course, gnawed at a piece of chicken and said, "Riches?"

"Franklin," Thomas said. "We're trying to find the lost fortune of the Lost State of Franklin."

"Lost fortune? Franklin?" Uncle Pickle said.

"You know about it, sir?" Thomas asked, almost panting.

"Why, sure!" Uncle Pickle replied. "It's the state that never got great. Heck, you got lots of things in Johnson City named for Franklin—there's State of Franklin Bank, State of Franklin Healthcare, the Franklin Woods Hospital, to name a few. And there's the State of Franklin Road, too."

"I know, sir," Thomas said. "And there's that shopping center."

"The Shoppes at Franklin," Uncle Pickle said, chewing on some chicken. "But, uh, heh. What makes you think there's a lost fortune?"

Thomas pulled the FRANKLIN TREASURY sign from his backpack.

Uncle Pickle took a quick look and said, "Hmmm, this thing smells funky."

"It's been in the mud," Zakk said. "We dug it out of the river."

"Err," Big Jon growled. "And that thing—that stupid board—it dug a splinter in my hand."

Thomas then told Uncle Pickle what he had leaned about Franklin: Early settlers had named this state for Benjamin Franklin, an elder statesman of the United States. They thought Mr. Franklin might lend support in turning Franklin into a real state, like North Carolina. But, as it turned out, Mr. Franklin hardly cared about the State of Franklin's formation, and Franklin died away—just before he did.

After lunch, the family stayed in Johnson City and, at Thomas's request, toured the nearby Tipton-Haynes State Historic Site.

*This is it,* Thomas thought, getting goose bumps as he crossed the site's grassy ground.

Whether Benjamin Franklin cared or not, he had missed his spot on the map thanks to what hap happened at Tipton-Haynes all those years ago, on February 27-29, 1788. On those days, gunshots rang out in a snowstorm, and there was utter confusion as Franklin's leaders—including John Sevier, the lost state's governor—slowly gave up a fight for statehood. Another pioneer, Evan Shelby, was slated to take the governor's chair on March 1, but Shelby refused, and the State of Franklin simply ceased to exist.

"This is the dark and bloody ground—if there is one for Franklin," Thomas muttered to himself.

A little later, Thomas got even more excited as he wandered the lawn with a local television news reporter, a dark-haired man with a mustache and a mole on his face. The reporter told Thomas that a tiny cave just off a wooded trail was once inhabited by early pioneers… and possibly a ghost.

"A ghost?" Thomas said as he walked inside the small cave.

Inside, the cave's walls appeared plain, pale, and almost like plaster. The ceiling was low—just about the right height for a kid to explore.

"If there is a Franklin fortune," Thomas said, his voice echoing in the cave, "it will surely be here."

"A fortune?" the reporter said, standing at the cave entrance. "No, not here. That cave has been combed clean and dry. If you want to know something, you need to go find out what happened after Franklin fell apart."

Thomas stepped out of the cave, and his glasses fogged up. He stood there, puzzled about what the reporter had said, while the rest of the family—Big Jon, Zakk, AnnaBelle, and Uncle Pickle—sat near a pond, not hearing a word.

"So, now where do we go?" Thomas wondered.

*Cave at Tipton-Haynes State Historic Site*

"Knoxville," the reporter said. "Go to Knoxville, Tennessee. The leader of Franklin, John Sevier, that's where he's buried. Or go to Rocky Mount. Go to that cabin. Find out about the Southwest Territory."

Thomas ran a few steps to meet his family at the pond, and he spelled out ideas for their next adventure.

"Rocky Mount?" Uncle Pickle said. "I know where that is."

"Yeah, that's just up the road," Big Jon said.

"Well, sort of," Uncle Pickle mumbled.

"But what about Knoxville?" Thomas said. "I mean, I think we should try there, sir. We need to find as many clues as we can."

"Knoxville?" Zakk said. "That's where I'm from."

"Can we go to the Knoxville Zoo?" AnnaBelle begged.

**To follow Big Jon and Thomas to Rocky Mount, turn to page 15.**

**To follow Uncle Pickle, Zakk, and AnnaBelle to Rocky Mount, turn to page 28.**

**To follow everyone to Knoxville, turn to page 50.**

# PINEY FLATS, TENNESSEE
## *Time Trip*

Rolling along with Big Jon in the Little Ranger, Thomas panted with excitement about getting to Rocky Mount. He had ideas of going back to the Tipton-Haynes State Historic Site, but Big Jon didn't want to hear about that—no, not right now.

Big Jon complained a mosquito had bitten his leg as he walked around the pond at Tipton-Haynes. "Couple that with the splinter from the Franklin Treasury sign," he said, "and I'm getting all beat up with you, Thomas."

"I'm sorry, sir," Thomas said. "But I do think it is high time that we get the necessary clues. I know there must be more— if we can just be smart about where to look."

"Smart," Big Jon muttered as he parked the Little Ranger at Rocky Mount, a living history museum and farm at Piney Flats, Tennessee. Here, a collection of cabins stood among rock outcrops, split-rail fences, and trees, all on the outskirts of Johnson City.

Still panting, Thomas approached a bearded man at the ticket counter and announced that he had been here before— as a student from an elementary school near his home in Abingdon, Virginia.

"So, you're a regular time-tripper," the man said. "You must really love history."

"Yes, sir," Thomas said, growing more red-faced with excitement. "We're here today to find out what happened to Franklin—the lost state. We have clear reasons to believe that it was not so lost after all."

"Err," Big Jon growled at the ticket taker. "Buddy, this kid'll talk your ear off."

"Yes, sir," Thomas continued. "And my cousin Zakk—we call him Zippy—he's going to be here any minute with my Uncle Bob, who, by the way, we have to call Uncle Pickle. And then there's AnnaBelle. Um, we just call her AnnaBelle.

Anyway, she's Uncle Pickle's daughter and another one of my cousins."

The ticket taker smiled. "So you're going to wait for all of them?"

"Yes, sir," Thomas said, clutching ever tighter to his big collection of papers as he wandered around the lobby at Rocky Mount.

Big Jon sat on the floor and chewed on his finger. Finally, after 20 minutes, he pulled out his splinter. After another ten minutes, he complained that the rest of the family must have gotten lost. So he pulled Thomas away from Rocky Mount's historical displays, and the pair went outside and started the tour.

They knocked on the door of the main cabin, where a costumed interpreter—a woman in her 50s—arrived. She explained that this was the home of William Cobb, a pioneer, and that the cabin had been built in the 1770s. She also indicated that this was the year 1791.

*Rocky Mount*

Thomas grinned. "Oh, sir," he said to Big Jon, "this is what I've been waiting for."

Looking at the woman, Thomas grinned even more and began, "What happened to Franklin? Was there a fortune lost, too?"

"Franklin?" the interpreter asked. "Oh, Benjamin Franklin—Big Ben. He died just last year, in 1790."

"No, ma'am. I mean, yes, ma'am," Thomas said. "But what we're really talking about is the State of Franklin."

"Oh, the state that died in infancy," the interpreter said. "We were a part of her—the old State of Franklin—as much as we were part of North Carolina."

"And now Tennessee," Thomas said.

"Tennessee?" the interpreter asked. "I know nothing of that name. We are now Gov. William Bount's headquarters for the Territory of the United States South of the River Ohio. But, of course, we just call it, 'The Southwest Territory.' And this, dear lad, is the year 1791."

Thomas paused. And, with that silence, Big Jon laughed, kind of enjoying the fact that his nephew was stumped for a response.

"Excuse me, ma'am," Thomas said, "but you know that this is really not 1791. I mean, I know that's part of your act, and that you have to talk in code, and that you have to keep your time trip intact. But if I could get you to break from all that… I mean… we might get some answers about Franklin."

"I know not what you say," the interpreter returned coolly, with a smile. "All I can say is that Franklin's fortunes have faded."

"Fortunes?" Thomas said excitedly. "So there really was a Franklin fortune? A treasury? Treasures? I mean, do you know anything about the cabin that was lost in 1897? Is it here?"

"In 1897?" the interpreter said. "My, oh, how I would only hope that the world would still be here, all those years from now."

Thomas stood silent, stumped again.

Then the interpreter winked at him and said, "I would try

Plum Grove—the home of John Sevier. Find that. John Sevier, he was our leader of Franklin. I would follow the path of Sevier."

"Yes, ma'am," Thomas said.

"And if it's a fortune you're looking for," the guide said, "do as we do here in 1791."

"Yes, ma'am," Thomas said.

She laughed lightly and said, "Go find a good cave and listen intently for the walls to tell you her secrets," With another wink, she left the pair standing at the doorway to the main cabin.

Thomas, now overloaded with information, stood entirely confused, saying he could not figure out where to spend the rest of the afternoon.

"I'd like to find Plum Grove," he said. Then he shuffled through his stack of papers and pulled out a brochure. "But what about here? This cave called Bristol Caverns… it's actually not far from my house in Abingdon… you think the fortune is here?"

**If Thomas and Big Jon go search for the site of John Sevier's house at Plum Grove, turn to page 23.**

**If Thomas and Big Jon go to explore Bristol Caverns, turn to page 19.**

# BRISTOL, TENNESSEE
## *Ghost of Betty Bishop*

Big Jon left Rocky Mount and a few miles later turned the Little Ranger down what he called "The Pea Picker Parkway"—a highway in Bristol, Tennessee, that was actually, and officially, named in honor of the late singer Tennessee Ernie Ford.

All during the trip, Thomas rambled excessively about growing up in Abingdon, Virginia, just a few miles north of Bristol. Excitedly, he told Big Jon about how he had stopped his bike on Plumb Alley in Abingdon and peered into the cave behind the Cave House on Abingdon's Main Street.

"They say all the caves are connected," Thomas said. "And inside? There must be secrets, sir. I know if I was a pirate of the mountains, I would have dropped all my fortune in a cave."

Big Jon tried to listen to Thomas and pay attention to the road at the same time, but he made a wrong turn down Route 421 and just kept on going, eventually ending up at South Holston Lake. He turned the truck around and, a half-hour later, finally reached the Bristol Caverns parking lot.

A dark-haired man began the underground tour for ten people, including Big Jon and Thomas. The guide held up pictures of the caverns and called them "images of America." Then he passed around a postcard and mentioned how city council meetings had been held among the cavern's stalagmites and stalactites.

"A long time ago, this was known as Bishop's Cave," the tour guide said. "It was named for Betty Bishop. She was beautiful, so beautiful. In fact, another woman was jealous of her beauty. That woman had Betty killed by two men. And later? The lifeless body of Betty Bishop was found in this cave."

19

"She was dead?" Thomas asked.

"Certainly," the tour guide said. "But sometimes, you can be very quiet—very still—and you can hear the ghost of Betty Bishop."

*Postcard of Bristol Caverns*

"A ghost?" Thomas shrieked.

"Err," Big Jon growled.

Then, as if he had been told a secret, Thomas whispered, "That's our clue, sir."

"Our clue?" Big Jon asked.

"She'll know," Thomas suggested. "Just wait. Wait here."

Thomas and Big Jon let the other eight guests go forward on the tour, and they stayed back, perfectly still, until everyone else had gone out of sight.

"Betty! Beautiful Betty!" Thomas said with a loud whisper that echoed off the cavern walls. "Betty, it's me—Thomas."

"Betty?" Big Jon asked, not whispering at all. Laughing loudly, he said, "Who knows you in this cave?"

"Betty Bishop!" Thomas cried with a loud whisper. And then, like he was singing, Thomas said, "Come out, come out, wherever you are!?

There was no reply. All Thomas and Big Jon could hear was the water of the Underground River.

Next, Thomas took a few steps away from Big Jon and continued to look at the ceiling, like he thought an image would appear.

"Betty, are you there?" Thomas asked. "Are you a ghost?"

## PLOP!

Thomas hunched down as he heard a large drop of water falling from somewhere in the caverns.

And then?

The sound of a scratchy shuffle seemed to come from the walkway.

A startled Thomas hid beside a rock. Closing his eyes and sobbing, he cried, "I'm sorry! Betty—I mean, Miss Bishop—I didn't mean to disturb you spirit... I mean, I just... I wanted to find... I mean, ma'am, I just—"

"Err....."

"AUGH!" Thomas screamed but then opened his eyes and saw... Big Jon!

"You silly squirt," Big Jon fussed, looking down at his hunched-up nephew. "C'mon Thomas. Cut out all the drama. Just who are you talking to?"

Thomas swallowed a tear. "I just thought we would talk... I mean, I guess we were having a séance," he said. "I wanted to talk to Betty Bishop—I mean, Miss Bishop—and I just thought she could tell me if she knew of any secret—"

"Fortune?" Big Jon said, snickering.

Thomas suddenly smiled and said, "Yes, sir. The Franklin fortune. I thought maybe I could get the ghost of Betty Bishop to tell me where it was."

"A ghost," Big Jon said. "You're talking to a ghost, Thomas?"

"Yes, sir."

Big Jon shook his head and growled again. "C'mon," he said. "Let's go."

If Big Jon and Thomas go to find Plum Grove, turn to page 23.

If Big Jon and Thomas go to Uncle Pickle's house, turn to page 67.

# ERWIN, TENNESSEE
## *Mountain Mystery*

All the roads of Northeast Tennessee started to look the same—going east, west, north, or south. And, after a while, it didn't matter how many times Thomas said he was sorry for getting Big Jon lost.

Turning left, right, and then back around, Thomas tried to lead Big Jon to the historic marker at Plum Grove, the site of a home of John Sevier, the first governor of Tennessee and, more important to Thomas, the only governor of the Lost State of Franklin.

But where was Plum Grove?

On the outskirts of Jonesborough, Tennessee, Big Jon complained that almost all of the Little Ranger's gas was gone. So Thomas gave his uncle $10, and they stopped to fill up the tank and ask directions.

A gas station attendant said Plum Grove was alongside the Nolichucky River, so the pair headed to Route 107. But along the way, Thomas had nearly glued his nose to his notes, and they ended up at Erwin, Tennessee, a small town just a short drive from Jonesborough.

And there?

Thomas swatted flies and flipped pages. He read aloud lengthy passages from Samuel Cole Williams's book *History of the Lost State of Franklin* and from a much smaller volume by Faith Stahl, "An Adventure in Northeast Tennessee."

Big Jon hardly listened; he talked about going to Uncle Pickle's house in Bluff City, Tennessee.

"Wait!" Thomas said, shuffling through more papers until his fingers grabbed something that Papaw—Big Jon's grandfather and Thomas's great-grandfather—had tucked away. It was a tattered brochure describing "The Unaka Mountain Auto Tour."

"This might be something, sir," Thomas said. "It's a loop."

"A loop?"

"It's a loop tour," Thomas said. "A driving tour in the national forest. It's here! It starts right here, sir, and it will get us right back here to Erwin."

Thomas quickly scanned the contents, reading the details of "Beauty Spot" and … a "secret mine."

"Secret mine!" Thomas suddenly shouted. "It's an old silver mine, sir. It says here, 'The productivity of the mine is unknown but was the subject of many discussions. The prospector who worked the mine traveled on foot through the villages below the mountain en route to his secret mine. It is said that he always returned with some silver.'"

"Err," Big Jon growled.

"Bingo!" Thomas shouted. "This could be it, sir. This could be our lost fortune. Oh, sir… please, sir. We have to make the loop."

"On the mountain?" Big Jon asked. "There's a road all the way around this Unicorn-what?"

"Unaka Mountain," Thomas said. "That's what this says."

He handed Big Jon the brochure. And, finally, Thomas convinced his uncle to follow the loop tour's series of curvy back roads and forest lanes.

They passed a place called "Indian Grave Gap." But Big Jon complained when he missed a turn and began driving down a maze of willynilly curves. The Little Ranger descended lower and lower into what Big Jon called "Nor' Ca'lina."

"North Carolina?" Thomas said, panicking. "We're going the wrong way!"

"This whole loop is the wrong way," Big Jon barked.

"Sorry, sir," Thomas said.

Big Jon headed back into Tennessee and turned right onto a skyward-spinning span of gut-grinding gravel. The lane was so narrow, it looked like a bike trail. Thomas kept silent and Big Jon groaned as the gravel attacked the under-carriage of the truck.

By now, Thomas was torn between fears for the pair's safety and the wonder of that lost silver mine: Could a fortune really be missing?

At an ear-popping elevation of 4,500 feet, however, Big Jon heard a horrible noise: a clearly audible *sssss* sounding like it was coming from a rear tire on the Little Ranger.

He stopped, and Thomas got excited.

"Good decision, sir," Thomas said. "We are still in the boundaries of the Lost State of Franklin. And, according to this brochure, I believe we have made it to the location of the lost silver mine."

"Err," Big Jon growled.

"What's wrong?"

Big Jon got out and found not one but two tires on his truck were losing air and going flat. He picked up his cell phone, but there was no signal; he could not call for help.

Thomas tried smiling.

Big Jon just laughed and said, "You know how we're getting back now?"

"Sir?"

"Shoe-leather Express."

Big Jon and Thomas started walking. They went two miles, mostly following the gravel road. Then they turned on a thorny trail and came to a crudely constructed cabin nestled in the woods. Thomas and Big Jon pulled back the creaky door and went inside.

It looked like somebody had lived there until recently. Big Jon made no comment on the cabin. He told Thomas to stay inside, adding, "I'm going to go play with my phone."

Thomas studied the cabin's construction. A few pieces of paneling were nailed to the walls. Yet it looked remarkably similar to what Thomas had seen earlier in Greeneville—the replica of the Lost State of Franklin cabin.

Sitting down at the center of the cabin, Thomas dozed off, exhausted from losing most of a night's sleep.

Thomas fell into a dream, and a mountaineer with a scraggly beard appeared, eating popcorn. "Boy, you got any sugar?" the man asked Thomas.

"Sugar, sir?"

"I used to live here—right here—in this cabin," the mountaineer said. "This is my home."

"Am I dreaming?" Thomas asked. "Are you a ghost, sir?"

"Yeah. I could be."

"Yes, sir."

"You don't know," the mountain man said. "I hauled this cabin up here on my back—half of it washed up on a river. I don't know where it came from. Just pieces—pieced it together from the side of the river and went upstream. Ain't nobody even know it's here."

"Upstream, sir?"

"Then came the flood—storm. Blew pieces of it off."

"Yes, sir."

"Must have been something. Why, to me, I think this cabin was at one time the capitol of something—where important people would meet, like a treasury—"

"Get up! Thomas suddenly heard Big Jon holler.

"Ouch, sir."

"Tow truck's coming," Big Jon said. "He says he knows exactly where we are."

"But your phone?"

"I walked up the hill. Found a signal."

"But, sir... this cabin," Thomas said. "I had a dream... I mean, I think—"

"I think it's a rat hole," Big Jon hollered.

"But, no, sir," Thomas said. "It was a real dream. It was so real. And this man—this mountaineer with a big, fuzzy beard—he talked to me. This is it, sir. This could really be—"

"A dream?" Big Jon asked. "Are we now over the rainbow?"

"Yes, sir" Thomas said. "I mean, no, sir. I mean, dreams sometimes give us clues. And I think this might have been it. The building. The capitol building. This cabin may contain the Franklin treasury."

"Thomas, I don't care what it is," Big Jon said. "All I know is, we've got only 40 minutes to meet the tow truck at the Little Ranger—and get out of here."

"But, sir!"

"C'mon!" Big Jon hollered. "Let's get out of here and go find Pickle."

**Turn to page 67.**

# FRANKLIN COUNTY, VIRGINIA

## *The Crooked Road*

Uncle Pickle told Zakk to get in the backseat of his tiny car, nicknamed "The Sally Saturn.: And then, after dancing around in the parking lot of the Tipton-Haynes State Historic Site, Uncle Pickle kicked the tires and drove away.

Ten minutes passed.

Zakk said, "There was a sign back there that said 'Rocky Mount.'"

"Rocky what?" Uncle Pickle asked.

"Rocky Mount," Zakk said.

"No, that's Rocky Top," Uncle Pickle replied. "You know, home sweet—Rocky. You know what I mean."

"But isn't that where Thomas was going?"

"You said Rocky Mount," Uncle Pickle said sternly. "And to Rocky Mount we shall roll!"

AnnaBelle smiled, sitting next to Zakk in the backseat. "My daddy's always right," she said, squeezing her Miss Brenda doll. "He's always right."

Zakk rolled his eyes and sank lower in the car.

Within an hour, Uncle Pickle had cruised into Virginia's Blue Ridge Highlands. He drove through a small town, and Zakk saw a man near a bicycle shop dressed as Santa Claus and smoking a pipe. Beyond that, Uncle Pickle navigated a particularly curvy road beside a tumbling stream crowded with fly fishermen. Quietly, he motored over mountains, passing Christmas tree farms, a river, and another small town.

Finally, after what seemed like forever, Uncle Pickle pulled into a gas station at a town called Galax.

"What is this?" Zakk asked. "Where is this?"

"The Crooked Road," Uncle Pickle said, smiling. "Look at this—the Crooked Road. We've been following this thing called the Crooked Road."

"Crooked Road?" Zakk wondered.

"Why, sure," Uncle Pickle said happily, almost singing his words. "It's got these cute little banjos on it—all these little signs. And you drive and you stop and you drive."

"But why?"

"Because you wanted to see Rocky Mount, Zippy Zakk," Uncle Pickle said sternly. "And to Rocky Mount we shall roll—over the escarpment and down the Crooked Road."

Uncle Pickle handed Zakk a brochure titled "The Crooked Road: Virginia's Heritage Music Trail." Zakk thumbed through the booklet, madly, almost ripping the pages. Then, in the middle, he found a map. He saw the lines of the "music trail" connecting towns across Virginia—from Hiltons to Bristol to Galax. There was also "Rocky Mount"—just like Uncle Pickle had said—and it sat in the middle of a place called... FRANKLIN!

"Franklin!" Zakk exclaimed. "Did they move it?"

"Move what?"

"Franklin!" Zakk exclaimed again. "We found it. I mean, is that what we were going to do?" Flustered, he said, "What were we going to do? Find Franklin? Is that where Thomas says the fortune is?"

"Fortune?" Uncle Pickle asked.

"Rubies?" AnnaBelle asked, clutching her Miss Brenda doll. "Are we going to find a ruby?"

"I dunno," Zakk said, sounding a little out of breath. "I mean, maybe. I mean, I think there's a fortune at a place called Franklin. That's what Thomas said. It's about that sign we found fishing. And now we're looking for a treasury—or a treasure, or something. We're looking for something."

"Ah," Uncle Pickle said, chuckling. "My boy, we're all looking for something."

Zakk looked at the Crooked Road brochure again. "Why does this say 'Franklin'?"

"That's a county," Uncle Pickle said. "It's Franklin County, Virginia. That's the end of the Crooked Road."

"And that's where the missing fortune is?" Zakk asked.

"I suppose," Uncle Pickle said. "I don't know what's missing or what's a fortune. But that's where we're going."

From the gas station at Galax, Uncle Pickle drove the Crooked Road for three more hours to Rocky Mount, Virginia. Finally he arrived at a motel, long after dark, and told Zakk and AnnaBelle to get to sleep.

The next morning, Uncle Pickle woke the kids up early, and they rode around the small town of Rocky Mount, where countless businesses used the name "FRANKLIN." Zakk, in the backseat, wondered if they had, indeed, found what they were looking for.

Then Uncle Pickle drove the Sally Saturn to the old train depot at Rocky Mount, and they got out to hear a group of musicians playing banjos, guitars, mandolins, and dulcimers. About 20 people stood around the depot parking lot, drinking coffee, eating biscuits—and clogging.

"I wanna dance!" AnnaBelle hollered and tore away from her father, waving her Miss Brenda doll high in the air.

Uncle Pickle chased his little girl. And so did Zakk. But Zakk did not care about the old-time mountain music, how fast AnnaBelle was dancing—or even if he got anything to eat.

"Uncle Pickle!" Zakk hollered. "When are we going to find the fortune?"

"Fortune?" Uncle Pickle said as he clogged, holding AnnaBelle's hand. "You're still on that? Oh Zippy Zakk—this is all the riches we need—this mountain music."

Zakk rolled his eyes. He moped over to an empty curb and put his hands on his cheeks, feeling lost.

And that's when he heard a voice.

"Sugarplum, I know you!" said a plump woman holding a mandolin.

Zakk looked up and said, "Huh?"

"I know you, little boy, but I can't make out why." The woman looked down at Zakk. "You're one of my sissy's kids, ain'tcha? But wait now—why are you here in Franklin?"

"Rocky Mount," Zakk mumbled.

*Rocky Mount Depot*

"Oh, really, you're in both," the woman said. "Rocky Mount is part of Franklin County."

Zakk signed heavily like he didn't care where he was. "I came with my Uncle Pickle and his daughter, AnnaBelle," he mumbled, holding his head down on his folded arms. "She's my cousin and—"

"Peanut butter!" the woman cooed. "Did you say Pickle was here?" The woman turned from Zakk and hollered "PICKLE!" across the parking lot.

By then Uncle Pickle was clogging in a trio, holding hands with AnnaBelle and her Miss Brenda doll. He looked up and yelled "MAGGIE!" across the depot's parking lot. He slipped away, with AnnaBelle and the doll, and ran to the woman, saying, "Sweet Magnolia, I thought we might find you here."

Maggie laughed and said, "This place gets me ready for my Franklin-to-Franklin run."

Uncle Pickle asked, "You still doing that?"

Maggie leaned a little closer to him. "I'm a berry runner," she said, trying to sound sly.

Zakk listened, but he paid attention to only one word in the odd conversation: *Franklin.* He asked about it, and Maggie cupped her right hand to grip his chin. He looked closely at Maggie's hands. They were purple!

Maggie noticed Zakk's stare and said, "I ain't contagious. Just been working on my farm over yonder in Floyd. I'll be heading to Franklin today."

"Franklin? Really?" Zakk asked. "Is there another Franklin?"

Uncle Pickle laughed and said, "You wanna go? You still looking for your fortune?"

Maggie laughed. "I'll get him to make one," she said, bumping Uncle Pickle's arm. "I'll put him to work, just like last year."

*Last year?* Zakk thought. And then it clicked: *This is Aunt Maggie.*

Aunt Maggie was Uncle Pickle's 33-year-old sister. She was also a sister to Zakk's mom, Thomas's dad, and Big Jon. She always wore a flannel shirt, even in the summer—an outfit that Uncle Pickle called her "costume." She usually wore a straw hat over her long brown hair, and on this morning she also had her hair wrapped in toiled paper, saying she had to protect her "five-dollar haircut."

Aunt Maggie lived on a blueberry farm in Floyd, Virginia, with her dog. *What's his name?* Zak thought. *It's a weird name. A funny name.*

"Well, decide!" Uncle Pickle exclaimed. "Zip to it, Zippy! You going back with us, or are you going on the Franklin-to-Franklin run with Maggie? You never know where your fortune lies."

If Zakk goes with Aunt Maggie to Franklin, turn to page 34.

If Zakk continues the trip with Uncle Pickle and AnnaBelle, turn to page 43.

# FRANKLIN, VIRGINIA
## *The Smell of Money*

Zakk climbed into Aunt Maggie's beat-up station wagon at Rocky Mount, Virginia, and found it stuffed with bushel baskets of blueberries. He also made friends with Aunt Maggie's dog; a big, fat, fuzzy mutt named Blob.

"Franklin?" Aunt Maggie asked.

"Franklin," Zakk said, smiling, as they pulled away. "There's a fortune to be found."

Aunt Maggie shook her head and laughed.

Nearly two hours later, they arrived in South Boston, Virginia, and stopped for a quick lunch. But Zakk was simply tired of the drive—and especially the smelly station wagon.

"Oh, honey," Aunt Maggie said. "we've got a long ways to go on this road—Route 58. I call this 'The Beach to Bluegrass Highway.' It goes from Virginia Beach to Kentucky's doorway at the Cumberland Gap. And today, it's going to take us all the way to Franklin."

"But what about Blob?" Zakk said. "He's back here eating blueberries."

Aunt Maggie laughed and said, "Well, Zakk, you have to teach that dog not to be like that."

"But I can't!"

"Oh, listen," Aunt Maggie said. "You better zip it, Zippy!"

Zakk sighed as Aunt Maggie kept driving, heading across Virginia on Route 58. Hardly saying a word, he just looked out the window as the hills, the houses, and the towns passed by: Clarksville, South Hill, Lawrenceville.

All along, Aunt Maggie cruised at 58 mph. "Going 58 on 58," she would say.

Then, after about 85 miles, Aunt Maggie looked in her rearview mirror and saw blue lights. She heard a whirring siren.

Blob started barking.

"Oh, sugarfoot!" Aunt Maggie shouted. "This always happens when I drive through Emporia!"

Aunt Maggie slowed her station wagon down and pulled it to the side of the road. A moment later, a police officer walked up to her window. Blob growled rather intensely, baring his teeth.

"Hey!" the male police officer shouted, looking into the station wagon. "You got that dog under control?"

"Why, yes!" Aunt Maggie said sweetly. "Honey, we've been rolling all the way from Franklin County, and maybe ol' Blob's a little—"

"Yuck!" the police officer suddenly shouted, pulling away from the side of the station wagon.

In all the excitement, and with a stomach full of blueberries, Blob lost his lunch: The dog threw up on the policeman!

"I am so sorry," Aunt Maggie said.

The officer shook his head and walked back to his patrol car. He came back a few minutes later and handed Aunt Maggie a speeding ticket.

She accepted it, quietly saying, "Thank you."

Continuing slowly along Route 58, Aunt Maggie stayed silent for an hour. Then, as she drove her station wagon into the gravel driveway of her tiny house in Franklin, Virginia, she handed the speeding ticket to Zakk and said, "This is going to come out of your pay, pal."

Zakk did not know what to say. He simply got out of the car and went into Aunt Maggie's garage to find an old skateboard.

The next morning, Aunt Maggie and Zakk went to the Franklin Farmers' Market on Main Street. On the way, Zakk complained about the station wagon's stench.

"Oh, honey," Aunt Maggie said. "That's the smell of money."

Zakk nodded, but he did not understand. He just rolled away on the skateboard in this city along the Blackwater River as Aunt Maggie set up her displays at the farmers' market. Zakk skated toward the Franklin train depot, built at the center of the small city around 1910. He also checked the time at a fancy clock standing on the sidewalk; Aunt Maggie had told him to be back in one hour.

*Welcome to Franklin, Virginia*

Grinning as he rolled the skateboard down North High Street, Zakk thought about how great it would be to find a "Franklin fortune," here, before Thomas found whatever it was he was looking for.

Aunt Maggie had said Franklin, Virginia, was likely named for Benjamin Franklin. So, Zakk figured, maybe that was a clue.

Skating again near the farmers' market, Zakk stared across Main Street at Fred's Restaurant, a downtown landmark, and he thought that the likeness of "Fred"—on a brick wall—looked a lot like Uncle Pickle.

Still staring, still rolling, Zakk—

**SMACK!**

-- slammed his skateboard into the clock on the Main Street sidewalk, just outside the Franklin train depot.

Falling down, Zakk held his nose and his right knee. He was hurt—not badly—but certainly too much to get back on his skateboard. Aunt Maggie heard him yelp, and she left her table at the farmers' market, running with a little package of blueberries in her hand.

Zakk muttered, "The missing fortune!"

Aunt Maggie stood over him, holding on to her blueberries, and said, "Your nose looks like a radish."

Looking up from the sidewalk, Zakk could only see Aunt Maggie's purple hands coming after him, getting ready to smash blueberries against his bloody knee and swollen nose.

"This will take the sting away!" she said loudly. "Blueberries will cure anything!"

*Franklin Farmers' Market*

Zakk felt like screaming. By now, he also wished he had never, ever heard the word *Franklin*. "I wanna go home," Zakk said, crying a little.

**If Aunt Maggie drives Zakk in her station wagon, turn to page 39.**

**If Aunt Maggie sends Zakk on a bus to meet Uncle Pickle, turn to page 43.**

# FRANKLIN COUNTY, NORTH CAROLINA
## *Gold Mines*

Waking up after a nap at Aunt Maggie's house in Franklin, Virginia, Zakk had a temper tantrum. He tossed a water balloon against her favorite blueberry basket. He tried to eat one of Blob's dog bones. He also put his hands on his hips and refused to move from the back door of the station wagon.

Finally, Aunt Maggie flipped over her nine-year-old nephew and gave him a spanking.

A day later, Zakk calmed down, and Aunt Maggie asked him why—why in the world!—was he so obsessed with places called *Franklin*.

"It's this board, this treasury board," Zakk said. "And Thomas. I really don't know. I wasn't paying attention."

"Does it have to do with Benjamin Franklin?"

"What? That long-haired man on the hundred-dollar bill? I guess so."

Aunt Maggie handed him a copy of Benjamin Franklin's book *Poor Richard's Almanac* and asked, "Will this help?"

"An almanac?" Zakk asked. "Is this about places to see?"

"Um, no," Aunt Maggie said. "These are common-sense things, to help you live better."

Zakk flipped through the book and found one line most intriguing: "Fish and visitors stink in three days."

The next day, Aunt Maggie loaded up the station wagon, ready to return Zakk to Uncle Pickle. Driving slowly down the highway, trying to avoid another speeding ticket, she turned her CB radio on and called out for any friendly voices. Just outside the small town of Courtland, Virginia, she heard her brother talking.

"Pickle!" she hollered. "Is that you?"

"Like a dill," Uncle Pickle answered through the fuzz of

static. "You still have The Zipster?"

Aunt Maggie laughed and replied, "Yeah, little Zippy took a beating from Father Time. Other than that, our Zipper Boy is just fine."

"It's 'Zakk!'" Zakk screamed from the backseat of Aunt Maggie's station wagon. "Stop calling me 'Zippy' and all those other dumb names."

Uncle Pickle laughed on the other end of the CB radio. "Oh, sounds to me like somebody is tired," he said, sort of singing his words.

Aunt Maggie asked, "What's your 20?"

"Outskirts of Nashville."

"Nashville?" Zakk said. "In Tennessee?"

Aunt Maggie asked, "Can you climb over to Medoc Mountain?"

"The park?" Uncle Pickle said.

"We'll get there soon," Aunt Maggie said. "Over and out."

"Is he in Nashville, Tennessee?" Zakk asked.

She did not answer.

About two hours later, Aunt Maggie pulled into the parking lot fronting the small office at Medoc Mountain State Park, a few miles south of Lake Gaston, North Carolina.

Within five minutes, Uncle Pickle pulled up in the Sally Saturn. He was wearing a miner's lamp on his forehead. Behind him, in the backseat, AnnaBelle was dressed in a golden outfit. Zakk climbed in, and the three took off.

"Daddy says you're homesick," AnnaBelle said. "I sure know we came a long way for you."

Zakk said nothing. Getting into the Sally Saturn again just seemed crazy, he thought. Uncle Pickle drove even slower than Big Jon. And, all along, he would stop to read historic markers on the side of the road.

Feeling quite bored, Zakk perked up when he saw a black-and-white sign pointing to Nashville. "What is that?" he said. "Are we in Tennessee?"

"Of course not!" Uncle Pickle said. "It's Nashville, North Carolina. And lookie there!" he said acting surprised as he stopped near a silver historic marker near the border of Franklin County, North Carolina.

"GOLD MINES!" Zakk shouted.

Both Zakk and Uncle Pickle got out to read the historic marker:

> ORE DISCOVERED AT FARM OF
> ISAAC PORTIS IN 1835; MINES IN
> THIS AREA PRODUCED NEARLY
> $3 MILLION BEFORE CIVIL WAR.
> LAST WORKED IN 1936.

*"GOLD MINES" of Franklin County, North Carolina*

"Is there still gold here?" Zakk wondered. "Is this another Franklin?"

"Another Franklin?" Uncle Pickle said, smiling. "Oh, Zip! Just wait until you see this one!"

Driving away from the historic marker, he rolled into a town called Franklinton, North Carolina, and pointed to a park and a library. Then he went another way, turning down a dirt road. Uncle Pickle parked his car and led a walk through some woods.

"As it turns out," he said, "this old gold mine has a seam—and a creek. I have called the landowner and gotten permission. We can stay here until your folks get back from Colorado. We can keep what we want... and look at this!"

AnnaBelle pulled a gold nugget from her tiny purse.

"Wow!" Zakk said.

"We could get rich," Uncle Pickle said.

"Oh, yeah?" Zakk said, smiling. "Just wait until Thomas hears about us! We found it! We found a Franklin fortune!"

## -- THE END –

# MARION, VIRGINIA
## *The Stranger*

After taking a detour to the bus station in Roanoke, Virginia, Uncle Pickle headed the Sally Saturn back toward Tennessee. Still, after traveling south for more than two hours, he could not resist stopping at a place with a name so intriguing that it made him think about lunch.

"Hungry Mother," Uncle Pickle said, just outside a state park in Marion, Virginia. "Why would you name a state park this? Why don't you just feed your mother if she's hungry?"

"I'm hungry," AnnaBelle said.

"Me, too," Zakk moaned.

So the trio grabbed some hamburgers at a tiny restaurant and drove to the lakeside beach at Hungry Mother State Park. There, beside a shade tree, the family saw a big man sitting on a bench and eating peppers from a can.

"Jah-lop-en-os," the big man said. "Here, you want to try some?"

"Heh," Uncle Pickle said. "Jalapeños?"

"Daddy, you always said, 'Don't talk to strangers,'" AnnaBelle chimed in. "Daddy, why are you talking to this stranger? Isn't he a stranger? Mister, are you a stranger?"

"Sorry," the big man said, eating another pepper.

Uncle Pickle grinned. "Well, where you from?"

"Marion," the big man said. "You?"

"Tennessee," Uncle Pickle said. "Bluff City."

"I'm from Knoxville," Zakk said. "And we're looking for the fortune—the Franklin fortune."

"Franklin?" the big man asked. "The State of Franklin? What? In Tennessee?

Zakk nodded.

"You know, that all got started right here," the big man said. "Arthur Campbell. You know him?"

"Oh, yeah," Uncle Pickle said. "I used to watch him on 'Hee Haw.' He had that cigar. Funny man, ol' Arthur Campbell."

"No," the big man said. "That was *Archie* Campbell. This is *Arthur* Campbell. He was a pioneer in the 1700s. And—little known fact—he was the one who wanted to start what became the State of Franklin."

"The lost state," Uncle Pickle said.

"Click!" the big man replied. "Back in 1782, it was Arthur Campbell's idea to get all these mountain areas—what are now parts of Virginia and Tennessee and Kentucky and North Carolina—and get them all grouped into another state. That didn't work, of course, but that's what people tried with Franklin. They took his idea, and they tried it around Tennessee."

"So?" Uncle Pickle said.

"So," the big man said. "So he had a house here. It used to be on Main Street—in Marion."

"Is it still here?" Zakk asked as a hint of thunder rolled across the sky.

The big man shook his head. "If I were you, I'd go someplace else."

"Someplace else?" Zakk asked.

"Like St. Paul," the big man said, smiling. "Ever heard of St. Paul?"

"Who is St. Paul?" Zakk asked.

"In Virginia?" Uncle Pickle said. "That town called St. Paul? Why go there?"

"I just would," the big man said as clouds suddenly blocked the sunlight.

"But why?" Uncle Pickle asked.

"I just would," the big man said again. "Look for the French Settlement."

"The French Settlement?" Uncle Pickle asked.

"Yeah," the big man said. "I just would."

Just then a clap of thunder made AnnaBelle jump. "I'm scared, Daddy," she said. "I want to go home."

44

If Uncle Pickle, Zakk, and AnnaBelle to to St. Paul, turn to page 46.

If Uncle Pickle, Zakk, and AnnaBelle return to Tennessee, turn to page 67.

# ST. PAUL, VIRGINIA
## *French Settlement*

On the advice of the stranger in Marion, Uncle Pickle traveled for two hours west to St. Paul, Virginia, with Zakk and AnnaBelle. There, they knocked on various doors, and, at a small office, they found a dark-haired woman with a pet monkey. Uncle Pickle asked her if she knew anything about any kind of lost treasure.

"Swift's silver mine?" the woman asked.

"Maybe," Uncle Pickle said, grinning. "We're looking for the Franklin fortune."

"Ben Franklin? The State of Franklin?"

"Yes!" Zakk said.

"Well, that's in Tennessee," the woman said. "And isn't that the name of a bank?"

Uncle Pickle smiled and prepared to leave, figuring he was at a dead end.

"Well, wait," the woman said. "Would this have anything to do with the French Settlement?"

"The French Settlement!" Uncle Pickle said, perking up. "Yeah. That's it. Some guy eating jalapeño peppers told us about it."

"Well, here," the woman said, handing Uncle Pickle a brochure for St. Paul's Sugar Hill Loop Trail. "You need to go see this. It's an old place, but it burned down—mysteriously—on Sugar Hill."

"Sugar Hill?" AnnaBelle asked. "Is that a whole hill of sugar?"

The woman laughed and said, "They used to make maple syrup on Sugar Hill. It's right across town, next to the little lake."

Loud thunder suddenly boomed, rattling the windows of the woman's office. Her pet monkey jumped to the floor and hid beneath a desk.

"Well," she said, "maybe you should just come back another day."

Uncle Pickle smirked. He took the brochure and headed across town to Sugar Hill.

More thunder roared as Uncle Pickle hiked with the kids, following a gravel trail for a mile along the Clinch River. Edging up a hill, the trio passed a small barn missing many boards, and Zakk suggested, "Maybe this is Thomas's long-lost Franklin cabin."

But they did not stop. Uncle Pickle simply used the brochure's map to finally reach the site of an old chimney and what looked like the foundation of a house. Nearby was a picnic shelter, and there the kids played while Uncle Pickle studied historic markers on the chimney.

The land was marked by tragedy. As early as the 1770s, a pioneer named John English had settled at this place. But in 1787, at the same time the State of Franklin had existed, Indians burst into the family's home and killed the man's wife and two young boys.

A few years later, the place became known as "The French Settlement" when it was occupied by a Frenchman, Francois Pierre de Tuboeuf. Soon after, though, thieves killed the Frenchman. And, many years after that, in 1976, vandals burned the structure.

Uncle Pickle turned from the signs and walked to the picnic shelter.

Then the rain came. A blinding rain landed in sheets, like a showerhead open at full blast. The kids huddled with Uncle Pickle in the picnic shelter as lightning crackled, the wind roared, and fog swept the grassy hillside.

Zakk started shaking. AnnaBelle cried.

The sky grew dark, and a heavy breeze rattled trees surrounding the shelter. Then the fog lifted, almost instantaneously, much like the rising of a curtain at a stage show.

Looking out across a field, Uncle Pickle and Zakk noticed

what appeared to be two young boys and a woman walking among tall grass.

"They don't even look wet," Zakk said.

Uncle Pickle scratched his head.

Then came another flash of lightning and more thunder. One boom popped so loud that it cracked everybody's eardrums. The fog returned quite suddenly and, within just a few seconds, became so thick that it was impossible to see anything beyond a few feet. The mist seemed to swirl strangely, like a hurricane or even a tornado.

From somewhere, an owl let out a hoot.

AnnaBelle screamed.

But then, in another moment, the swirl of wind dissipated and the fog disappeared.

And in the distance?

"Nothing there," Uncle Pickle said.

"Where are the boys?" Zakk asked. "Where's that woman?"

"Did they get lost?" AnnaBelle said.

"Or were they ghosts?" Zakk asked.

Uncle Pickle signed and said, "Guess what else is gone."

"What?" Zakk asked.

"The map," Uncle Pickle said, frowning.

Within minutes, the rain stopped, and Uncle Pickle announced it was time to start walking again. AnnaBelle lasted only a few steps. She stopped, and Uncle Pickle and Zakk took turns carrying her.

They turned left, just beyond the French Settlement, and walked for about a mile. They made another left turn and came to the Clinch River. Yet Uncle Pickle's decision to make another left turn and then another landed them right back where they had started—at the picnic shelter.

By then, it was dark. The three spend a restless night huddled together at the picnic shelter. AnnaBelle cried, too, as she heard coyotes howling in the distance, sounding like sirens.

The next morning, they all started walking again. But this time, Uncle Pickle made every intention to follow the path that brought them to the French Settlement in the first place.

In little more than an hour, the trio finally made it to the safety of the Sally Saturn. Driving away, all made a pact: They would never again go hunt for lost fortunes nor would they hike when they heard thunder.

AnnaBelle also made one more rule: Beware of the advice of strangers.

## -- THE END --

# KNOXVILLE, TENNESSEE
## *Golden Globe*

Big Jon drove his truck to Knoxville, Tennessee, and met Uncle Pickle at a restaurant for ice cream. Then the whole family drove away in Uncle Pickle's tiny car, the Sally Saturn, with Big Jon at the wheel.

Zakk sat in the middle of the backseat, saying he was excited because they were in his hometown, Knoxville.

"Yes, but Knoxville is on the fringe of Franklin," Thomas said, shuffling through his stack of papers. "We're going deep into Tennessee to get here. I'm not sure this area was even considered part of the Lost State."

"So?" Zakk said. "We can still go see the Big Orange."

"The football team?" Big Jon asked.

"No, sir, we can't, sir," Thomas said. "We need to head downtown—to the Knox County Courthouse. We need to see the grave of John Sevier, the governor of the Lost State of Franklin."

Uncle Pickle and Thomas each tried to give Big Jon directions to the courthouse. But Big Jon got lost and ended up traveling down Henley Street.

"What's that?" AnnaBelle asked, pointing out her window to a giant tower.

"The Golden Globe?" Uncle Pickle said.

"Oh, that's the Sunsphere," Thomas said. "It was built for—"

"Err," Big Jon growled. "It looks like a big disco ball."

"Yes, sir," Thomas said. "It's from 1982. It was built for--"

Zakk interrupted this time, saying, "I always wanted to go up in that tower."

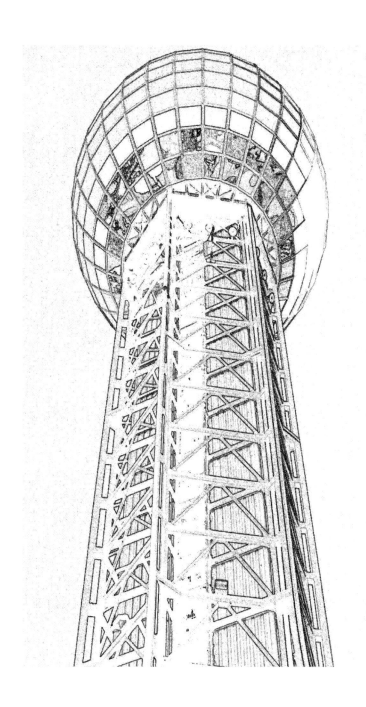

"I want to go!" AnnaBelle cried. "It looks magical, like a fairy tale. And look at the top, Daddy. It's full of gold!"

"No, ma'am," Thomas said, clenching his notes. "That's the Sunsphere. It has nothing to do with John Sevier. It's not exactly an historical—"

"The World's Fair!" Uncle Pickle shouted, like an explosion. "That's why they built that tower. That was quite a deal for Knoxville in 1982."

"World's Fair. Yes, sir," Thomas said quietly, speaking to no one in particular. "The Sunsphere, it was built for—"

"Gold!" AnnaBelle cried. "There is a treasure here. Look at the gold, Daddy. Hey, Thomas, we found your treasure. Aren't you happy? Now my daddy can buy me the biggest ruby ever."

"But, wait… no," Thomas said. "The Sunsphere—" He stopped talking as, finally, he realized no one was listening.

Big Jon parked the car, and all except Thomas ran to the Sunsphere tower. Thomas lagged behind, feeling misunderstood, and ultimately decided to just stand outside the car, reading his notes about the Sunsphere.

Built for the 1982 World's Fair, the 266-foot-tall tower was made to symbolically represent the sun—with a diameter of more than 86 feet and window glass panels layered in 24-carat gold dust.

"But we can't keep the gold!" AnnaBelle said, stamping her left foot after returning from the family's visit. "The gold is on the windows, and it has to stay on the tower forever."

"So what!" Zakk said. "Let's go find the Big Orange."

"But I want to go to the zoo!" AnnaBelle cried.

"No, ma'am," Thomas said, getting in the Sally Saturn. "We have to go see John Sevier."

Once again, no one listened to Thomas.

Big Jon drove to the campus of the University of Tennessee and the giant Neyland Stadium, the home of the Volunteers— or "Vols"—the beloved UT football team. And here, Zakk said, is where the family would find the Big Orange.

"But where is it?" Zakk found himself saying.

Everyone shrugged.

"The Big Orange!" Zakk said, exasperated. "There is supposed to be a big orange here."

"What do we use it for?" Big Jon said, laughing. "To make orange juice?"

"Good grief!" Uncle Pickle said. "'Big Orange' is the nickname for the football team."

"No," Zakk said. "It's a—I mean, I thought there really was a big orange here."

"Err," Big Jon said, growling again. "So, like, if you go to New York City, you think there's gonna be a big apple?"

"Oh, very funny, sir," Thomas said, laughing a little. "But back up in Bristol, close to my house, sir, there is a very big guitar. Actually, it's called the Grand Guitar. And it's right on the highway—the biggest guitar ever."

"Well, let's go there then!" Zakk said, trying not to feel defeated.

"No!" AnnaBelle cried stubbornly. "I want to go to the zoo."

"Stop it!" Thomas suddenly shouted and let out a big puff of air. He threw his hands high and screamed, "Sevier!"

Big Jon laughed. But Uncle Pickle heard that fit and knew the only way to cure Thomas: It was time to get back on the course of finding Franklin.

After that, Uncle Pickle grabbed the wheel of the Sally Saturn and drove to the Knox County Courthouse, where Thomas spotted the gravestone monument of John Sevier, the first governor of Tennessee and the only governor of the State of Franklin. Panting excitedly, Thomas jumped out of the car and snapped some pictures. : Look" he said, making notes. "This says John Sevier was nicknamed 'Nolichucky Jack.'""

Trying to speak to the spirit of Franklin's governor, Thomas knelt at the base of the monument. "The Nolichucky," he said, "that is the river where we found your sign, sir. Is that your sign? What was the Franklin Treasury?"

No answer came.

"Are you here, sir?" Thomas stared at the gravestone. "Speak to me, sir. Can we feel your presence?"

*Gravestone of John Sevier*

Again there was nothing.

"C'mon, Thomas," Big Jon barked. "Get up. You're acting like a cow patty."

Thomas did not listen. He simply closed his eyes and breathed heavily. Then he tilted his head back and said, "The river."

"The river?" everyone wondered.

"We need to return to the Nolichucky River," Thomas said. "Nolichucky Jack says the Nolichucky River holds Franklin's secrets."

No one said a word—well, at least for a minute.

Then came a question from Zakk: "Is this John Sevier guy the same thing as Sevierville?"

"In Tennessee?" Uncle Pickle said. "Oh, yeah, Sevier County and Sevierville—they were both named for John Sevier."

"Well, isn't Sevierville next to Pigeon Forge?" Zakk asked.

"Pigeon Forge?" Big Jon asked.

"That's Dollywood," Uncle Pickle muttered.

"Dollywood!" Zakk said. "We need to go to Dollywood!"

**To follow Thomas's suggestion to go to the Nolichucky River, turn to page 61.**

**To follow Zakk's suggestion to go to Dollywood, turn to page 56.**

# PIGEON FORGE, TENNESSEE
## *Silver Dollar City*

The whole family crammed into Uncle Pickle's car, the Sally Saturn. It was a tight squeeze—and hot. But nobody cared, not even Thomas. Everyone was simply excited about heading to Dollywood, the Tennessee theme park named in honor of singer and superstar Dolly Parton.

"Dollywood is in Sevier County," Thomas announced. "According to some of my sources, this area was also part of the Lost State of Franklin. Meaning, if there was a Franklin fortune—and I believe there was—the fortune could have been here, too."

"Righto!" Uncle Pickle shouted from the driver's seat.

AnnaBelle smiled and giggled. She happily bounced her Miss Brenda doll, tapping it on the back of Big Jon's head a couple of times. "Miss Brenda likes you," she said.

"Err," Big Jon growled.

All the while, AnnaBelle stared intently at the theme park's entrance signs. She noticed all of the butterfly symbols of Dollywood and said, "I like Dolly Parton's song—'Butterfly Kisses.'"

"That's not her song!" Zakk snapped. "Her song is called 'Dog and Butterfly.'"

"You ding-dongs are both wrong," Big Jon said. "Dolly Parton's big hit was 'Muskrat Love.'"

Thomas laughed. But he bit his tongue, trying to stop laughing. "Dolly Parton's famous song is 'Love is Like a Butterfly,'" he said. "That was the reason they put all the butterfly signs around the park here."

"Righto!" Uncle Pickle said again.

The family spent close to two hours exploring the rides of the theme park. But then, after crashing on the bumper cars,

Uncle Pickle stood motionless inside Dollywood's Country Fair with a serious look on his face.

"I know this says Dollywood," he said. "I know this place belongs to Dolly Parton. But I really believe there was something else here."

"Huh?" Zakk said.

"There is more to it," Uncle Pickle continued. "Seems like, once upon a time, this was something different. This was a mining camp—some kind of working man's place. This was a place where men slaved to make a fortune. It was hard work and tough times. Floods and fires."

"Huh?" Zakk said again.

"Dolly Parton," Uncle Pickle announced in a heavy tone. "I know for certain that she was not the first to walk these grounds."

"What do you mean, sir?" Thomas asked.

"Just go this way," Uncle Pickle commanded, leading a charge into a Dollywood tunnel connecting the Country Fair to the Dollywood Grist Mill.

All of the family followed, and they passed a gem mine operation along the way.

Inside the dark tunnel, AnnaBelle asked if there were any rubies to be found. "And George Washington," she said. "Was George Washington here?"

Uncle Pickle said nothing to his daughter. He simply stopped walking and pointed to a sign on one of the tunnel's dark walls. It was a drawing noting the story of "The Miners of Silver Dollar City, Tennessee"—with a description by W. R. Warburton, dated 1879.

"This is it," Uncle Pickle said.

"What is it?" Zakk asked.

"This is the clue," Uncle Pickle said. "The smoking gun. This is all of the above. See how this sign says, 'the miners are the unknown and mostly unseen.' So there! That proves that this place was not always about Dolly Parton."

"What?" Big Jon said.

*The Miners of Silver Dollar City*

"It wasn't," Uncle Pickle said sternly. "This was Silver Dollar City. I know it was. And I know, if we keep looking hard enough, we will find clues like this to indicate the real story."

"The real story?" Thomas asked. "Could this have to do with the Franklin fortune?"

"That's what I intend to find out," Uncle Pickle said, grinning. "And I also intend to find just what they did with all that silver dollar stuff." He turned and walked out of the tunnel, disappearing into the theme park crowd.

Shrugging, the rest of the family went on to explore more rides. Just as everyone boarded an indoor roller coaster called Blazing Fury, all in the clan were suddenly surprised to hear a familiar voice—crying "FIRE IN THE HOLE!"—as they rode into the darkness.

It was Uncle Pickle! He was now working at Dollywood!

"Actually, I'm more like a secret agent," Uncle Pickle explained later. "And this place, friends—Blazing Fury is one of the original rides. It's a landmark. And if you look around right here, you'll see what I'm talking about—all kinds of signs pointing to Silver Dollar City. It's even marked on the building outside."

"So?" Zakk said.

"So I intend to stay here the rest of the week and find out what they did with all the silver dollars," Uncle Pickle said.

Thomas raised his hand. "They simply changed the name, sir," he said. "Once upon a time, this was a theme park called Silver Dollar City, and now it's Dollywood. It was changed for Dolly Parton. I asked one of the managers while you were gone."

Uncle Pickle laughed sarcastically. "You believe that, don't you?" he said. "Well, you and Zippy Zakk can believe that all you want. But there was a reason—there must have been— why this was even called Silver Dollar City in the first place."

"What?" Zakk said.

"Oh, I will find the answer," Uncle Pickle said confidently. "Who knows? It could be the richest silver mine ever lost in

Tennessee. And the Lost State of Franklin, Thomas? A fortune? Hmm, there could be some silver dollars here that nobody ever remembered."

"You're gonna stay here all week?" Big Jon bellowed, scrunching up his face. "What are we gonna do all week while you're working?"

"Ha!" Uncle Pickle said, digging into his pocket. "I gather you'll have a lot of fun while I'm conducting the search for Thomas's fortune."

"What do you mean, sir?" Thomas asked.

"I'm mostly a volunteer," Uncle Pickle replied. "But I did manage to get this job by making a deal: I got us a place to stay, meal tickets, and free passes to Dollywood."

Everyone cheered—even Big Jon.

## --THE END --

# DANDRIDGE, TENNESSEE
## *Catastrophe*

All Thomas could talk about was "The River." For some reason, and though he could not explain it, he had felt that the spirit of John Sevier, the governor of the State of Franklin, had talked to him. And now Thomas did not want to go anywhere else. The only way to reach the "Franklin fortune," he insisted, was to go back to "The River."

But Big Jon complained and refused to return to the fishing spot on the Nolichucky River where Thomas had found the FRANKLIN TREASURY sign. Big Jon said he was afraid he would get another splinter.

So, as a compromise, Thomas settled on going with Big Jon and Zakk to explore the shore of Douglas Lake at Dandridge, one of Tennessee's oldest towns. Uncle Pickle and AnnaBelle, meanwhile, decided to spend the rest of the day at home in Bluff City, Tennessee.

Situated between Greeneville and Knoxville, Dandridge took its name from Martha Dandridge Custis Washington, the wife of President George Washington. The area's landscape changed in the 1940s when the Tennessee Valley Authority built Douglas Lake near Dandridge, impounding the channel of the French Broad River to form a giant watery playground.

Riding along with Big Jon in the Little Ranger, Thomas and Zakk studied the land near the lake. Pines, maples, and large oak trees grew amid patches of scattered grass and sticker vines. At one fork in the road, Thomas motioned Big Jon to follow the direction pointed by a crude sign announcing "SUBMARINE."

Big Jon shook his head but drove down the road anyway. A mile later, near a sign that simply said "SEE," Zakk and Thomas motioned Big Jon to stop, and the boys jumped out of the Little Ranger.

Thomas and Zakk skipped over scattered logs and stepped around a sprawling fig tree. They ran another 200 yards and approached a cinder-block building, covered with buoys, nets, bamboo, a couple of anchors, several large barrels, buckets, and another sign that read "SUBMARINE RIDES."

Zakk burst open the door of the tiny building and went inside. The stinky shop was crowded with fragments of old cars and boats, several flotation devices, and what looked like the sides of an old ship.

"You really have a submarine?" Zakk shouted.

"Can we really go down inside the lake?" added Thomas, just as excited, as the two boys stared at Darnell "Dandelion" Jones, a burly, middle-aged man with a beard.

Wearing a captain's hat, Dandelion told the boys that he was a tinkerer and explained, "I got me this here submarine from the Navy."

"Can we find treasures?" Thomas wondered.

Dandelion laughed and said, "You never know what you'll find. People lose everything."

The boys paid $10 each for a ride with Dandelion, and they walked down to a dock where Dandelion had parked his four-seater submarine on Douglas Lake. In all the excitement, however, the boys forgot to run back and tell Big Jon where and with whom they were going.

Squeezing inside the tiny vessel, Dandelion told the boys not to touch anything. "I do all the controls," he explained.

Soon after, the trio departed the dock and slowly slipped below the surface of the lake. Dandelion flipped a switch that turned on a spotlight at the front of his submarine, allowing a slightly better view of the reservoir's grainy, muddy surface.

The lake looked dark and lonely—even eerie—as they cruised above the bottom covered with sunken cans, tires, rocks, tree limbs, chairs, fishing lures, and a vacuum cleaner.

"You could do a lot of salvaging down here with this stuff," Dandelion said.

"Sir," Thomas said. "Um, how much of this lake is

downstream of the Nolichucky River?"

"All of it," Dandelion said. "The Nolichucky joins the French Broad to make this lake."

"So any treasures from upstream near Greeneville might have washed down here?" Thomas said.

"Probably," Dandelion said. "What I like is this big ol' catfish down here. I call him Catastrophe. And he's down here in this—lookie here."

Dandelion pointed out the submarine window to an old Volkswagen Beetle, a red car with broken windows. It sat permanently parked on the bottom of the lake, covered with moss, mud, and tangled fishing lines. It was—in one word—dirty, having been lost in the lake for several years.

Yet there, hovering above a board on the backseat, was Catastrophe—a five-foot-long catfish wagging its tail.

## WHOMP!

The entire car shook, like it was dancing in its submerged spot.

"Hey—look at that," Dandelion said. "That's worth yer ten bucks for this tour alone. Now, let's see if I can get 'er down a little more."

The submarine continued to sink lower, lower,..... lower.

## CLANK!

The submarine became snagged on the sunken Volkswagen. Dandelion, in a sweat, worked his controls and furiously tried to push a lever to go back up.

"Oh, no, sir!" Thomas panicked. "We're stuck, sir!"

"Shake it!" Dandelion shouted.

Thomas's glasses fogged up in the humidity, and he lost his balance.

Dandelion pushed against the submarine's walls, and the submarine started to shake. But Thomas, unable to see, slammed his head against a switch—and passed out.

Dandelion screamed, "You better start shaking!"
"What?" Zakk said.

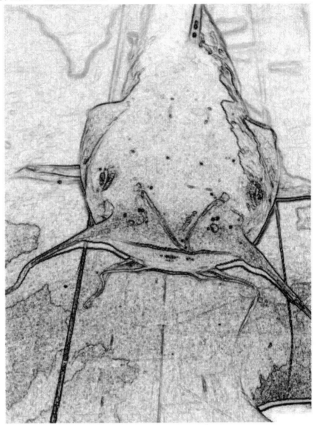

*Catastrophe the Catfish*

"Shake it!" Dandelion screamed again.

Zakk did not understand. He panicked, too, as tiny drops of water seeped into the submarine.

Dandelion made more mad jerks at his gears. But it seemed to no avail. The submarine remained, unfortunately, fastened to the car.

"Shake it!" Dandelion screamed.

Then, as if on cue, Catastrophe the Catfish wagged his tail.

The entire Volkswagen moved. And, with it, so did the submarine.

Huge bubbles arose at the bottom of the lake, along with a dust cloud so thick that it became impossible to see anything outside the submarine's window.

"Shake it!" Dandelion screamed.

Catastrophe the Catfish shook the car again.

## WHUMP!

The submarine broke loose. But Dandelion, so relieved, forgot to turn down the high level of his gears.

## WHOOSH!

The submarine shot straight off the bottom of the lake, rising like a rocket to the surface, splashing and buoying itself on a wake as powerful as an ocean current. Dandelion let the submarine bounce as the waves dissipated. Then he turned the vessel and, without a word to Zakk, headed back to the dock.

Big Jon stood waiting, with a frown. He never saw the boys leave, but he had watched the submarine's sudden ascension to the surface, and he knew that splash could not be normal.

"What happened?" Big Jon barked as Dandelion popped out of the submarine's door hatch.

"We got too close," Dandelion said with heavy breaths.

"Too close?"

Zakk popped out of the hatch. "I think Thomas is dead," he said.

"Dead?" Big Jon bellowed.

"Ah, he ain't dead," Dandelion muttered.

Big Jon brushed past Dandelion and went to the submarine's door. With Zakk's help, he got Thomas out of the submarine and sat his motionless body on the dock. Big Jon could tell his nephew was still breathing, but Thomas just wouldn't wake up.

"What's wrong with him?" Big Jon asked.

"The little feller bumped his head," Dandelion mumbled.

"For what? Going to see all this Franklin stuff?" Big Jon shouted.

Hearing Big Jon's words, Thomas whispered, "Franklin."

"No more Franklin!" Big Jon said, leaning down and slapping Thomas's cheeks.

Thomas blinked his eyes and said, "I guess we are—"

"—in big trouble," Big Jon said. "You guys never did tell me where you were going."

"But—" Zakk said.

"That's it," Big Jon said.

And so it was. The quest for finding Franklin was over.

Big Jon made Dandelion give the boys a refund for their tour. But, as a punishment to Thomas and Zakk, Big Jon confiscated that $20 and put it toward gas in the Little Ranger.

Next, he headed back home to Greeneville and made the boys work in the yard for three straight days. And on the third night? They had a bonfire—and Big Jon burned the FRANKLIN TREASURY sign.

# --THE END --

# BLUFF CITY, TENNESSEE
## *What is a Dinah Shore?*

Big Jon and Thomas waited inside Uncle Pickle's house in Bluff City, Tennessee, for what seemed like forever. Then, finally, Uncle Pickle, Zakk, and AnnaBelle rolled across the Reed H. Thomas Memorial Bridge on Boone Lake, and Uncle Pickle parked his small car at his house along Main Street near the Thomas Hardware store.

"Where have you been?" Big Jon barked as Uncle Pickle and AnnaBelle got out of the Sally Saturn.

"Rocky Mount," Uncle Pickle said, grinning. "Where were you?"

"Rocky Mount!" Big Jon said. "We were there. You never showed up."

"Well, it's a big town," Uncle Pickle said, shaking his head. "I guess we went to one place, and you went another."

"Rocky Mount is not a town, sir," Thomas said. "It's an historic site."

"Well, no," Uncle Pickle said slowly, sounding agitated. "It seemed like a town to me."

Thomas went on, "Did you go in the cabin, sir?"

"What cabin?" Zakk asked.

"We went to the train station," AnnaBelle answered. "And we heard all this beautiful music. And we saw Aunt Maggie. Sweet Magnolia."

"Maggie!" Big Jon hollered. "Our sister, Maggie? What is she doing in Tennessee?"

"Tennessee?" Uncle Pickle said. "She was in Virginia."

"Virginia!" Big Jon shouted.

"Virginia was not really part of the State of Franklin, sir," Thomas said. "I mean, except for how it all got started with Arthur Campbell. My research says he lived in Virginia, at

67

Marion, and it was his idea to start a state, as early as 1782, and join up with the other settlers of the mountains. This was all-"

"Virginia," Uncle Pickle said, turning away from Thomas and looking at Big Jon. "We went to Rocky Mount, Virginia."

"Err," Big Jon said. "You would go around your elbow to get to your ear."

Uncle Pickle sighed and said, "What's that supposed to mean?"

"Rocky Mount is in Tennessee," Big Jon said. "It's not even ten minutes from here in Bluff City."

"See!" Zakk exploded. "That's what I told you!"

Uncle Pickle sighed again and, with AnnaBelle, walked toward his house.

Laughing, Big Jon walked the opposite direction along Main Street with Zakk and Thomas. Going a couple of blocks to the old bank building of Bluff City, Big Jon and the boys turned down J. Forrest Thomas Street, near Bluff City Elementary School, and soon arrived at a small house belonging to Mr. Taylor, a 70-year-old retired welder.

"You boys ready to mow?" Mr. Taylor asked.

"What?" Zakk said. "What do we have to do?"

"Cut the grass," Thomas said. "Mr. Taylor is going to pay us."

Zakk and Thomas promptly began mowing the lawn. Mr. Taylor and Big Jon, meanwhile, talked about restaurants that served chicken. Mr. Taylor also fiddled with the radio in his garage as Big Jon made a list of places where he wanted to go eat.

Exhausted after mowing the lawn, Thomas and Zakk stood panting a while later, and they looked at Mr. Taylor, much like puppy dogs expecting a treat.

Mr. Taylor handed each boy a dime and said, "Off you go."

The boys stood speechless. Zakk, for one, seriously wondered if he and Thomas had slaved for half the afternoon in the lawn for a mere ten cents apiece.

Then Mr. Taylor laughed, and so did Big Jon, and Mr. Taylor handed each boy a $10 bill.

*Old Bank Building of Bluff City, Tennessee*

Zakk got excited, and he stayed that way even as Thomas said, "The Franklin fortune will give us much more."

"More than $10?" Zakk said. "Uh-uh. This is a lot."

Thomas sighed. Sure, he liked earning money, but something nagged at him. He knew—he just knew!—a fortune could be found.

Clearly, Thomas was frustrated after having read all about Franklin—and practically all places called Franklin. He had continually searched for more clues to unravel the mystery of the FRANKLIN TREASURY sign. He was convinced a clue might be at Nashville, Tennessee—the place where the State of Franklin cabin was shipped for Tennessee's centennial exhibition in 1897. Or maybe, he thought, the original cabin ended up at Franklin, Tennessee, or even Franklin County, Tennessee!

"Hold it," Thomas said. "Who is singing this music?"

"Oh, that's Dinah!" Mr. Taylor shouted, trying to make himself audible over the loud radio in his garage. "Dinah Shore!"

"Dinah Shore?" Zakk asked. "What is a Dinah Shore? Is it a beach?"

"It's a person," Thomas said. "Oh, I mean *she's* a person, sir. She's a singer. I mean, she's from Franklin. She's a Franklinite. I mean, maybe she's not one of the original Franklinites from the original Lost State of Franklin. But she's from Franklin County in Tennessee. And maybe this is a sign, sir."

Big Jon jumped up, saying, "A sign?"

"It's a sign that we should go to Franklin County," Thomas said. "We need to see where Dinah Shore came from."

"Franklin County?" Zakk muttered. "I just came back from Franklin County."

"What are you talking about?" Big Jon said.

Thomas, ignoring both, fumbled through his papers—by now having grown into a great glob of tattered pages copied from books plus handwritten notes and crinkled brochures. Thomas carried his Franklin notes everywhere, even to Mr. Taylor's house.

"Here!" Thomas exclaimed. "It says right here that Dinah Shore was born in Franklin County, Tennessee! Another Franklin! And don't you think it's curious, sir, that Mr. Taylor is listening to Dinah Shore?"

"Heh," Big Jon said. "He listens to anything."

"But, wait," Thomas said, shuffling through his papers once more. "Ooh!" he shouted, suddenly getting more excited. "It says here—right here—that the original Franklin County jail burned down, and the current Franklin County Jail Museum was built in—" Thomas swallowed hard and said, "It was built

70

in 1897."

"Err," Big Jon said.

"In 1897!" Thomas said again. "Don't you get it? That's the year the centennial celebration took place, and the original Franklin cabin was moved, and who knows? I know. That's where we need to go! Franklin. Let's go to Franklin County. We're going to find the fortune, and we're going to be rich."

"No," Big Jon said. "I ain't dragging you to any more of your places. Not on your, er, dime. The only place we're going now is Nor' Ca'lina."

"North Carolina?" Zakk said.

"But, sir," Thomas pleaded. "We need to go to the other Franklins. Either that, or we could go back to the river where we found the sign. Or we could go to Knoxville and see where John Sevier is buried."

"I think we should go to someplace fun," Zakk said. "Like Dollywood."

"Nope," Big Jon said. "We're going to Shatley Springs. Gonna get me some chicken."

"But what about Uncle Pickle?" Thomas said. "Would he go to the other Franklins?"

"Err," Big Jon said. "If you go with that guy any place in Tennessee, he'll probably end up in Nor' Ca'lina anyway."

**If Thomas asks Uncle Pickle for a ride, turn to page 76.**

**If Thomas convinces Big Jon to go back to the river, turn to page 61.**

**If Thomas convinces Big Jon to go to Knoxville, turn to page 50.**

**If Zakk convinces Big Jon to go to Dollywood, turn to page 56.**

**If Big Jon gets his way and goes to Shatley Springs, turn to page 72.**

# SHATLEY SPRINGS,
# NORTH CAROLINA
## *Lost Province*

Big Jon drove Zakk and Thomas through a series of Tennessee towns—Elizabethton, Shady Valley, and Mountain City—before slipping into Ashe County, North Carolina. They stopped briefly at a garden store, and Thomas picked up a book about this hard-to-reach area in the northwestern corner of the Tarheel State.

"This is the Lost Province!" Thomas shouted from the book aisle.

Ten people inside the garden store looked at him.

"They call Ashe County the Lost Province because it's so hard to reach," Thomas said, speaking loudly. "Oh, no! Now I'm thoroughly confused. This book says Ashe County became part of the State of Franklin in Eastern Tennessee and Western North Carolina. Was Franklin here, too—in North Carolina?"

Big Jon walked over to Thomas and shook his head. Saying nothing, he simply led his nephew back outside.

A half hour later, Big Jon drove the Little Ranger to Shatley Springs Inn, a well-known restaurant in Ashe County. Inside, Big Jon sat down for an all-you-can-eat feast of country ham, whipped potatoes, hot biscuits, vegetables, and his favorite, fried chicken.

The boys ate lunch, too. But Big Jon never stopped eating as they walked outside and studied the grounds at Shatley Springs, including the restaurants' free spring water, believed to cure all kinds of skin diseases, stomach ailments, and nervous disorders.

The boys then picked up a brochure for a place called "The Blowing Rock" and ran to find Big Jon, now munching on his fourteenth piece of chicken.

"Let's go here!" Zakk shouted.

"Err," Big Jon said, then polished off one more drumstick.

Arriving about two hours later at the Blowing Rock, a tourist attraction in the High Country of North Carolina, the boys found a 20-foot outcrop on a cliff that curves about 1,500 feet above the Johns River Gorge.

Here, tradition says, an Indian girl fell in love with a brave from a neighboring tribe. But they were not allowed to be together. So the young brave jumped from the cliff—only to be blown back into the arms of the girl he loved!

"Do people still jump and see if they blow back up?" Zakk asked.

"No!" Big Jon said emphatically.

"I think we're supposed to toss hats from the Blowing Rock," Thomas said, "and see if they blow back up. But, um, sir... I think, Big Jon, you're the only one who has a hat."

"Err," Big Jon said. "Don't even think about it."

"But, sir!" It works, sir!" Thomas said. "It's like defying gravity. The wind blows through this gorge, and your hat will come back."

"Forget it," Big Jon said, sitting down on the Blowing Rock cliff and rubbing his stomach. "Aren't you supposed to be finding Franklin or something like that?"

At that moment, a gust of wind rushed up and blew Big Jon's hat off his head. Zakk ran to retrieve it. Then, with laughs, Zakk and Thomas practiced tossing Big Jon's hat from the Blowing Rock. Each time, they watched the hat blow back as incoming winds funneled through the gorge and hit the bottom of the Blowing Rock.

Big Jon hollered about his hat—just once—then nodded off in the cool breeze. Awake again after a few minutes, he mumbled, "Time to get back to Tennessee."

"Franklin?" Thomas said, anxiously.

"But what about here?" Zakk asked. "Maybe somebody dropped something and it didn't blow back. There could be a treasure."

*The Blowing Rock*

"Oh, Zippy!" Thomas said. "We need to concentrate on the Franklin fortune. And I, for one, am not convinced that Franklin was really in North Carolina. The fortune, as I believe there is one, lies in Tennessee. So that's it. We need to go to Knoxville and find the grave of John Sevier. Or we need to go back to the river, where we found the FRANKLIN TREASURY sign."

"Why can't we just go back to Papaw's farmhouse in Greeneville?" Zakk said. "I'm tired of riding in all these cars. This summer is turning out to be too much road work."

"Oh, Zippy!" Thomas said again. "We need to go."

If Thomas convinces Big Jon to go to Knoxville, turn to page 50.

If Thomas convince Big Jon to go back to the river, turn to page 61.

If Zakk convinces Big Jon to go back to Greeneville, turn to page 80.

# FRANKLIN, NORTH CAROLINA
## *Ruby*

Logic! Landmarks! Luck!

*Augh!* Thomas felt frustrated—almost defeated—like he was on the verge of finding Franklin and uncovering a fortune, but no one understood what he was talking about.

So, after leaving Zakk and Big Jon at Mr. Taylor's house, Thomas marched through the tree-lined streets of Bluff City, carrying his stack of Franklin papers. He made his way back to Uncle Pickle's house on Bluff City's Main Street and asked his uncle to help him search for the Franklin fortune.

"Why me?" Uncle Pickle said. "All you guys do is make fun of where I drive."

"But, sir!" Thomas pleaded. "You know Franklin. I know you do."

"I do," Uncle Pickle said slowly, looking Thomas up and down.

"Well, sir," Thomas said. "Let's join forces and put an end to this mystery."

Thomas shook Uncle Pickle's hand. And, within minutes, they left with AnnaBelle in the Sally Saturn.

Uncle Pickle drove west to downtown Kingsport, Tennessee, where he began making a seemingly endless rotation at Church Circle, driving around and around the traffic circle while AnnaBelle giggled.

Thomas was not impressed.

"We have a long way to go to get to Franklin," Thomas said. almost impatiently.

"I know that," Uncle Pickle said, sounding testy. "We're going out the back way—it's a shortcut to Knoxville. And, from there, we can hit any road and get to Franklin County or

Franklin."

Hardly more than two hours later, the Sally Saturn rolled into rush-hour traffic at Knoxville, Tennessee, passing signs for I-40 and I-75.

"Asheville or Nashville?" Uncle Pickle hollered at Thomas, who sat in the backseat.

"Nashville!" Thomas said, struggling to speak in the wind blowing through the car's open windows. "Franklin is just below there. And during the centennial celebration, the capitol was on display in Nashville."

"He said 'Asheville,'" AnnaBelle said.

"Asheville? This way?" Uncle Pickle said, not turning his head.

"Nashville!" Thomas said.

"Asheville! Nashville!" AnnaBelle said, trying to sing "Asheville! Nashville!"

And, with that, Uncle Pickle headed east on I-40, driving for dozens of miles. Along the way, the sun sank in the western sky, and Thomas and AnnaBelle dozed off.

By nightfall, Uncle Pickle had gone about 100 miles from Knoxville. Yet, then, he discovered he was now driving through North Carolina—not Tennessee.

Pulling over in a restaurant parking lot, Uncle Pickle fumbled through Thomas's papers and found a map of the Eastern United States. He pinpointed his location, near Lake Junaluska, but he decided not to turn around, because getting to either Franklin or Franklin County in Tennessee would consume too much time.

So, instead, he headed south on Route 23. And, then, in little more than an hour, he woke the kids and said, "Okay, we're here. Let's check into this motel."

"Franklin?" Thomas said with sleepy eyes.

"Franklin," Uncle Pickle returned.

And yes, they were in Franklin. But this was actually Franklin, North Carolina!

Waking up late the next morning, Uncle Pickle took the kids for a walk. At lunchtime, the three passed a sign at the

Franklin Town Hall on Main Street.

"Augh!" Thomas said. "Uncle Pickle, sir, we're supposed to be in Tennessee!"

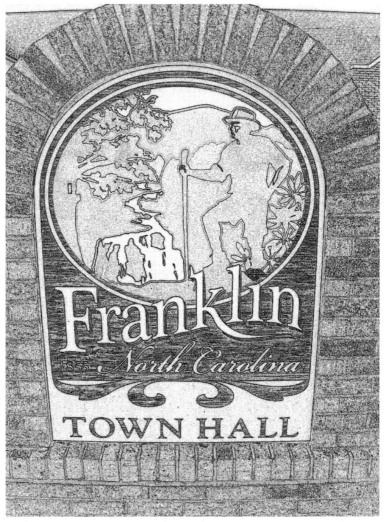

*Welcome to Franklin, North Carolina*

"Asheville! Nashville!" AnnaBelle sang again. "Hey, look Thomas!" She pointed to Franklin's town hall sign, showing the drawing of a man with a walking stick, standing near waterfall. The sign also used a diamond-shaped jewel as the dot for the "I" in Franklin.

Next, AnnaBelle glanced across Main Street and noticed signs for Ruby City—a museum and gem stone shop.

"I want a ruby!" AnnaBelle begged.

"Where are we?" Thomas asked.

Uncle Pickle grinned and said, "Well, it is a place called Franklin. Only, it's not the Franklin where you wanted to go."

"But how did we end up here in North Carolina?" Thomas wondered.

"Um, never mind that," Uncle Pickle said. "The important thing is that we're all partners in finding Franklin—and a Franklin fortune."

"But, sir," Thomas said, "I was looking for the lost cabin and the Lost State of Franklin. It has to do with the treasury sign. I have all these clues and—"

"Well, you're here now," Uncle Pickle said, again sounding testy.

"And there are rubies!" AnnaBelle said, gleaming from ear to ear.

Reluctantly, Thomas followed Uncle Pickle and AnnaBelle through town. They visited the Franklin Gem and Mineral Museum on Phillips Street, and they discovered this Franklin was called "The Gem Capital of the World." All around the forested mountains of Franklin, prospectors had discovered garnets, emeralds, sapphires, and rubies.

Later, Thomas, AnnaBelle, and Uncle Pickle sifted through raw ore in a gem mine near Franklin. Thomas's glasses fogged up as he worked in the water of a flume, but he cherished his newfound gems. He even convinced Uncle Pickle to stay another day at Franklin, North Carolina, so he could look for a new kind of "Franklin fortune."

As for AnnaBelle, she cared only about the treasure she found in Franklin—a giant ruby!

## --THE END –

# GREENEVILLE, TENNESSEE
## *The Garden*

Going back to Papaw's farm in Greeneville felt like a big letdown for Thomas. "We need to get to Nashville—and see where the Lost State of Franklin capitol building stood," he begged. "And West Virginia! I read about another place. It's called Franklin, and they have a Treasure Festival there every year. Franklin. It's a place called Franklin."

"West Virginia?" Big Jon asked. "You're nuts. You don't have enough money to pay my gas to West Virginia."

Zakk laughed.

"Well, at least Zakk got to go to the Franklin County in Virginia," Thomas said and stamped his right foot on the ground. "I never got to go hardly beyond the Lost State of Franklin."

Big Jon laughed but only for a second. "Ah, c'mon," he said. "You're acting like you did when AnnaBelle threw your toys down the toilet."

"No, sir," Thomas said. "I'm acting on all this research. And I know—I just know—that there is a Franklin fortune. It makes sense. The cabin is gone. And it never came back. So there must have been a treasury or a treasure. And—"

Thomas stopped talking. He sat down, feeling exhausted, frustrated, and defeated. Looking around the yard, his eyes grew heavy. He yawned.

In a minute, he was asleep.

An hour later, Thomas awoke, still shaded by the apple tree where he had slept. For a couple of minutes, he sat in a daze, yawning some more. Then his eyes caught Big Jon, digging the garden.

Big Jon handed Thomas a shovel. "Dig this new spot," he said. "I want to put a compost here, and we'll turn it into a garden next year."

Thomas nodded and started digging.

More than 15 minutes passed, then a half hour. Thomas never stopped digging—until...

## CLANK!

He hit something.

"Ah, rats!" Big Jon hollered. "What'd you bang into? The septic tank?"

"I don't know, sir," Thomas said. "But it is made out of metal." He leaned down and carefully pulled back great mounds of dirt. Gradually, he could see more and more of a box. His heart raced. The metal container—buried more than two feet below the surface—appeared to be olive drab in color and about 30 inches long.

It took Thomas almost 15 minutes to get the dirt away from it. Then he sat the box on the grass.

"I'm going to clean it up," he said. "I think it's—" At that moment, Thomas suddenly thought of something Old Man Dan had given him—something that had belonged to his great-grandfather, Papaw, the country doctor.

Thomas rushed inside the farmhouse and fumbled through his suitcase. He pulled out a small bag of assorted stuff—his dime from Mr. Taylor, a white clay marble, and the key from Old Man Dan!

Thomas went outside, and Big Jon and Zakk watched as he slipped the strange, old key into the metal box, and ...

## BING!

The lock opened. Inside the box, Thomas found crinkled pages from a newspaper dated November 28, 1939. Then he pulled out a small velvet sack, neatly folded inside the metal box.

He unwrapped the sack and instantly found himself face to face with—Benjamin Franklin!

The sack held a bundle of $100 bills—some folded, some bent, some crumpled. There were ten—no, a dozen—no, dozens. Maybe a hundred! Thomas unwrinkled more and more. There were so many $100 bills that he lost count.

And there was a note, scribbled in old-style, fancy handwriting, with the word *treasury*—plus part of a poem, saying, "If I could fish all day, I would not worry about pay."

"This is it!" Thomas exclaimed.

"It must have belonged to Papaw," Big Jon said. "Look—that's his handwriting."

"There is a Franklin fortune after all!" Thomas said, grinning.

"Yeah," Zakk added. "Sometimes, treasures are buried in our own backyard."

## -- THE END --

# EPILOGUE
## *The Lost State of Franklin*

For the settlers of what is now East Tennessee, the idea to form a new state called "Franklin" simply grew out of frustration.

North Carolina had ceded its westernmost area—between the Appalachian Mountains and the Mississippi River, including the newly formed counties of Sullivan, Washington, and Greene—to the federal government in 1784 to help pay its share of debt incurred during the Revolutionary War.

Residents of the mountainous region immediately grew afraid of having no government at all. So they borrowed an idea from Arthur Campbell, a Virginian who had proposed in 1782 that a new state should be formed from regions that now make up Virginia, Kentucky, Tennessee, and North Carolina. Several men met at Jonesborough, Tennessee, in 1784 and made plans to form a new state. They elected John Sevier, a native of Augusta County, Virginia, as the governor.

Initially called "Frankland," an Anglo-Saxon term meaning "Land of the Free," the infant state within months became "Franklin"—for political purposes—when organizers thought they might enlist the help of Benjamin Franklin, a senior statesman of the newly formed United States of America.

Where was the State of Franklin?

Largely, the state existed in what is now East Tennessee— from Bristol on the Virginia border to present-day Blount County, just east of Knoxville. That would include the counties of Hawkins, Sullivan, Johnson, Carter, Washington, Unicoi, Greene, Hamblen, Jefferson, Cocke, Sevier, and Blount. Though the exact boundaries remain unclear, some historians claim that Franklin also included parts or all of Hancock, Claiborne, Grainger, Union, and Knox counties, along with sections of western North Carolina in the High Country of Ashe County.

The capital moved from Jonesborough to Greeneville in 1785. But Franklin faded by 1788. Two years later, the State of Franklin region became part of the Territory of the United States South of the River Ohio—better known as the Southwest Territory—which in 1796 became the State of Tennessee.

What happened to the State of Franklin's original capitol building? Therein remains a mystery. According to tradition, the old log structure in Greeneville was dismantled in 1897, piece by piece, and hauled by wagon to Knoxville. Then it was shipped by barge from Knoxville to Nashville for Tennessee's centennial celebration, which was held a year late because of a lack of funds.

The whereabouts of the building are unknown after the exhibition. The logs were possibly discarded or stolen. Still, another story says a great flood hit Nashville, and pieces of the cabin were simply swept away by water.

A replica of the Lost State of Franklin capitol, built in Greeneville in 1966, stands today as a memorial to a short-lived state that never won its place on Ol' Glory.

This photograph made in the late 1800s in Greeneville, Tennessee, shows what some historians believe to have been the original capitol building for the State of Franklin. The structure was shipped to Nashville in 1897 and disappeared after the celebration of the Tennessee Centennial. Some historians debate, still, whether this was actually used as the real capitol building.

# ABOUT THE AUTHOR

Author Joe Tennis is descended from several generations of pioneers at Greeneville, Tennessee, the capital of the real-life Lost State of Franklin in the 1780s. As a Radford University graduate, Tennis has contributed articles and photos to *Blue Ridge Country*, the *Bristol Herald Courier, Appalachian Voice, The Roanoke Times*, the *Kingsport Times-News*, and *The Virginian-Pilot*. He has also written for *Virginia Living*. His other books include *The Marble and Other Ghost Tales of Tennessee and Virginia, Beach to Bluegrass, Sullivan County Tennessee, Haunts of Virginia's Blue Ridge Highlands*, and *Southwest Virginia Crossroads*.

Made in the USA
Columbia, SC
07 July 2021

41309619R00052